HART

EVIE MONROE

Copyright and Disclaimer

This book is a work of fiction. The names, characters, places and incidents are products of the writer's imagination and have been used fictitiously and are not to be construed as real. Any resemblance to persons, living or dead, actual events, locales or organizations is entirely coincidental.

Table of Contents

Hart

Steel Cobras MC Book 5

By Evie Monroe

HART

Chapter One

Hart

The Steel Cobras stared at Jet like he'd grown a horn on his head.

Jetson "Show-No-Mercy" Nash, Steel Cobras' Sargent at Arms, the kid who hated Hell's Fury more than any of us.

Had he lost his fucking mind?

We were all on edge. It had been a shitty night. We'd gone out with plans to dispose of Slade's body, the Hell's Fury president we offed trying to save his daughter from his wrath. To make it work, we had to keep it under wraps, but a Hell's Fury newbie had seen us. We couldn't let him go and squeal on us, so we brought the skinny kid in as our hostage.

So Cullen, our Steel Cobras President, had called church with the purpose of finding out what the hell we were going to do with the dickhead, now that we had him tied up in our clubhouse.

My first thought? Kill him. We weren't in the business of playing nice with the Fury. We weren't running an orphanage here, especially for boys who'd made the mistake of choosing our rival gang.

As long as I didn't have his blood on my hands, I didn't care. I had better things to do.

Of all the guys, I thought Jet would be most in agreement. For the past year, he'd been ready to go out killing, every time anyone even brought up the Hell's Fury.

But in the past week, he'd changed. The rumor was, he was shacking up with a sweet little doctor. Leave it to our pretty-boy Jet to get a girl who was well above his pay grade. Now, he seemed almost . . . *soft*.

Maybe I didn't hear him right. I pretended to clean out my ears, cupped my hand around the ear closest to him, and leaned in. "What did you just say?"

He shrugged. "I think we should let him live."

Cullen had the same thought I did. We were all a little Twilight-Zoned out, especially since it was well after two in the morning. He raised an eyebrow at Jet. "You feeling all right, Jet?"

Drake, who was thick as thieves with Jet, the peanut butter to his jelly, gave him a knowing nudge and murmured, "What? Did the old ball and chain tell you that?"

Another thing I'd been thinking. Then again, it could've been his brush with death. He'd taken a bullet in the stomach during the raid at Slade's place.

Jet just grinned. For our youngest officer, he had balls. Wasn't afraid of ruffling feathers and getting in people's faces. From the moment Phoenix, our Vice President, had introduced him to me as a prospect, I didn't like him. Too cocky. Arrogant. And liable to get us all into trouble.

What could I say? I was the safest one in the club.

Which, in a bunch of yahoos like this, wasn't saying much. But I calculated, thought things through. I didn't like to play the odds.

Drake started to taunt him, and I joined in, just because the pretty-boy deserved it. I said something about him not wanting to break a fingernail, and Drake made the same comment about him not wanting to mess his hair up.

Usually, that got Jet riled, but now he just ignored us. Looked like that girl of his had finally made him a man.

While we were laughing about him finally popping his cherry, he cut us off. "—Look. I think I have a better way."

Our eyes all went toward the kid, who was sitting in the corner of the warehouse, tied to a chair, a sullen expression on his face. In the shadows behind some of the rides we'd lifted, he was too far away to hear our conversation, but he was watching us, with a mixture of fear and suspicion. He hadn't moved much all night, except now his head hung lower and the circles around his eyes had darkened to huge black rings that looked like he'd been punched.

"All right. We'll get to that," Cullen muttered. "First order of business is Slade."

Right. Slade. We didn't take killing men lightly, but Slade was one asshole who'd had it coming. We'd all done a little victory dance when he got offed. Jet and Nix had gone off, trying to make his death look like the Cobras weren't involved, so that the war between us wouldn't reach a fever pitch. The kid in the corner had been our one complication.

We'd been led on a high-speed chase all through the streets of Avalon Bay, California, trying to evade the police while keeping the kid from getting to the Fury and blowing the whole plan.

We were all waiting to find out if our little plan to dump Slade's body had worked.

"Police found him last night. It was all over the news. Haven't heard so much as a buzz from the Fury but I'm hoping them not retaliating on us yet is a good thing. But that's not saying they won't come after us, even if they don't think we're responsible for Slade. They hate us, and we hate them, and this war ain't over."

We all nodded solemnly.

We'd been in a war with Hell's Fury for a long time. They'd been trying to take over our business of lifting cars for our partners overseas for as long as I'd been part of the Cobras. But it'd just about reached a boiling point. Blood was being shed every few months on both sides, little skirmishes, with the real battle yet to come.

We knew it was inevitable, but Cullen was biding his time to make sure we were fully prepared, in order to limit our casualties as much as possible.

"Second order of business." Cullen hooked his thumb over his shoulder, toward the kid. His name was Joel or something. Wasn't yet out of his teens, I'd say. Didn't look much like MC material, but hey—we'd all been there. I'd been the fat kid with glasses before I hit puberty—pushed into every locker in middle school. Good thing I'd grown out of that shit.

The men leaned forward. "So tell us," Nix said, looking at Jet. "What is it? I'm pretty sure, Jet, that you're the one who wanted to show the Fury no mercy just last night. So why should we let him live, knowing what he knows about us?"

He grabbed a pack of Marlboros off the table and tapped one out. He brought it to his lips. Keeping us in suspense, the cocky asshole. "Because we can use him. He's worth more to us alive, than dead."

"How?" Zain asked.

"Simple. We turn him. To our side."

The men looked from one to the other. *Simple.* Sure. Jet was probably still on pain meds if he thought it was that simple.

Cullen nodded his head slowly, and asked the other thing we were all thinking: "Simple? How? That's impossible. How do you plan to do that?"

"It's possible," Jet said, pointing at Zain. "Zain—"

"In case you didn't notice, we didn't have Zain tied up in our clubhouse as our hostage all night before he defected to our side," Cullen muttered. "This guy? Joel? He don't like us very much. And I don't blame him."

"Plus," Nix interjected. "Did you forget, baby brother? He was *shooting* at us."

Zain looked over at the kid and stroked his chin. "I don't know. It could work. It all depends on—"

"Look," Jet said. "What do we know about him? He's new to the area. Doesn't even know his way around. Was off on his own. Doesn't look like the Fury was taking good care of him. If we show him what it is to be in a real club, it could . . ."

"You know," Zain said, clapping Jet on the back. Great, that was all Jet needed to feed his big ego. "Jet has a point. The guys in the Fury were shits to me when I was prospecting. We could feel this kid out and see."

Jet and Zain fist-bumped across the table.

"I think we should. We should at least give it a chance," Jet said.

The men nodded.

Christ. I didn't know about this. I would have felt safer just offing the kid and moving on. But I didn't want to be the one putting a bullet in his head. None of us did. We weren't cold-blooded killers. So I reluctantly lined up on Jet's side. "All right. I mean, he is just a kid."

"All right," Jet said, slamming his hands on the table. "Let's vote and get this over with!"

Cullen gave him a look. "Who the fuck are you callin' for a vote?"

Cullen tolerated Jet because he was Nix's little brother, but the guy could get on people's nerves. He was always trying to take over Cullen's job. Finally, he said, "All right. Who's for it?"

Zain, Nix, and Jet all raised their hands at once. Drake and I followed.

Finally, Cullen lifted a finger. "Fine. We'll just test him out first. But if it ain't workin', we come up with another plan."

Jet flashed a smug grin. He probably expected the kid to get down on his knees and kiss his feet. Then he got up out of his chair. "Gotta go, guys, I've got someplace to be."

We all stared at him. He always thought he could float in and out of this place like a fucking movie star. No one ever kept him in check. If it was up to me, I'd have kicked his out ass long ago.

"See you later, ladies," he said, pulling open the door and making his exit.

"Elvis has left the building," I muttered.

Zain tipped the ash off the end of his cigarette and scrubbed a hand over his face. "More like he has some pussy to be in."

"This meeting over?" Nix asked.

Cullen nodded and the guys started to get up. I closed the top of my laptop and looked over at Joel, who was staring at us with his lip raised in a snarl. "What about the kid?"

Cullen motioned to Nix and Zain. "Put him in the storage closet for now."

I didn't like the sound of that. I watched as the two guys grabbed him under his arms and hauled him to a closet where we kept a bunch of random shit and tossed him in. The kid let out an "oof" as they closed the door. Nix locked it and brushed his hands together.

I shook my head. "Sure. Let's throw him in the storage closet. That's a great way for us to turn him to the Cobras. Hell, we'll be his heroes after spending the night in there."

Cullen crossed his arms. "You have a better idea?"

I frowned. I didn't. But I didn't like how King Jet breezed in here with his half-assed plan, got us to agree with him, and then breezed on out, expecting us to clean up after him. This had the makings of disaster all over it.

"Yeah," leaning forward in earnest. "Let's not tie him up. Let's just talk to him and reason with him. Maybe we can get some intel out of him."

Cullen listened to me, nodding his head, so I could tell he agreed. "You didn't think we should kill him. Right?"

"That's what I said."

"Why?"

I glanced at the closet where we'd dumped the kid. "At first, I did. I thought we should just get rid of him. We don't need the complication. But he's just a kid. I sure as hell didn't know what the fuck I was doing when I was his age."

Cullen took the end of his cigarette and sucked on it, then stubbed it out in the ashtray. "You joined the Cobras when you were just a kid."

I shrugged my shoulders. The point? "But it was dumb luck I didn't end up on the other side. I probably could've, just as easy, if the Fury had chosen the Lucky Leaf as their garage."

The Lucky Leaf was my dad's garage. Most of the Cobras worked there and brought their bikes in to get fixed. I'd grown up watching the guys come in with their bikes, each one tougher than the next . . . and even when I was that fat kid with glasses, I knew what I wanted to be. A Cobra. I got my first bike when I was fourteen and grew up into the club.

He pointed at me. "Then you'll be perfect for this."

I snapped my eyes to him. "For . . .what?"

"For watching the kid. Taking care of him. Getting him to *like* us, senator."

Senator. That was a nickname Cullen sometimes used for me. He said I was like a politician. Likeable. Diplomatic.

My mouth opened, and for a second, nothing came out. "You're fucking kidding me. I'm not a fucking welcome wagon."

"Yeah. But otherwise we'll have to kill him."

"Okay. But why me? What about Jet? This was his bright idea. Let him—"

He clapped me on the back. "But you're a likable guy. You have more charm than any of us. If we let Jet do it, you know what would happen? The kid would end up hating us more and beg the Fury to kill us. Jet rubs people the wrong way."

I let out a big breath of air. Zain always told me I should run for office. He said I was nice. Too nice, obviously, since it was pretty obvious where I was about to finish.

Dead last.

Fuck.

"You can keep him in line, right?"

I muttered under my breath and grabbed my helmet as I watched the rest of the guys slip out the door.

"Listen," Cullen said, quietly in my ear. "Can you put something on his phone so we can track his calls to the Fury?"

That, I could do. In addition to being the club *nice* guy, I was also the club *tech* guy. What he was asking for? He knew I could do it. I'd done it before. "Not a problem."

"So go in there and talk to him and see what you think. If you think you can work with him, do what you want. Don't leave him in the storage closet. Take him home with you. Give him something to eat. Whatever you think. We trust your judgment."

Great. Fucking great. Last thing I needed was this kid to be my shadow. I liked my apartment the way it was. Liked living on my own. This was for shit. But somebody had to do it, and the rest of the guys had already left for the night. So I guessed I was the sucker. "Got it."

I took a step toward the closet.

"And Hart," he said, his voice turning even more serious. "If the kid tries to get away from you or gives you any indication he ain't playing by our rules. You have our permission to put a bullet in his head."

Right. Let the nice guy kill the kid.

"Turn off the lights and lock up when you leave, okay, Hart?" Cullen said to me as he stepped outside.

I nodded and shoved my helmet back on the counter. I guessed I wasn't going to be going home any time soon.

Yeah, I was definitely too nice. How'd I let myself get talked into this shit show?

I walked over to the door and opened it. It was pitch black inside. As light flooded in, I saw the kid lying curled up on the ground like he wanted his mama. He lifted his head to look at me as I came in, his eyes pleading.

I grabbed him and hoisted him up, setting him down on a chair in the back of the room. I loosened the gag down over his chin.

He unleashed a stream of curses into the air and started to shout for help.

Fuck. I pulled the gag up so I could think for a second.

"Listen to me," I said, leaning down. "You can use a fucking bullhorn if you want. You are too far away for anyone to hear you. So don't waste your breath."

He stopped growling and moaning like a dog and looked at me, eyes narrowed, trying to be a tough guy.

"Now. I'll take the gag off, if you'll talk to me like a reasonable person. Okay? That's all I want to do. Talk. Can you do that?"

He gazed at me warily and then nodded.

I pulled the gag down. He didn't speak.

"Okay. Now that we've established that . . . can I get you anything? Beer? Water?" I asked. Christ. Listening to myself, I felt like I was in a parallel universe. Never thought I'd see the day when I was offering refreshments to the Fury.

The kid sniffled a little. "Water."

I left the room and returned a few minutes later with a bottle of water. I motioned to the ties on his wrists. "If you won't be an asshole and try to escape, I'll untie you."

He hung his head. "'s all right. I won't."

I grabbed the knife from my jeans and cut the ropes behind his wrists. His posture loosened, and he relaxed as I handed him the bottle. He downed it in big, thirsty gulps. When it was empty, he crunched it and handed it back to me and wiped his mouth with the back of his hand.

Then he looked up at me through his mop of dark hair.

I leaned against the wall. "So tell me. What did you see, when you were out in that field by the gas station?"

He shook his head. "I ain't seen nothin'."

I crouched in front of him at eye level. "You saw nothing?"

He nodded, and a smile spread over his lips. "Yeah."

"Then why the fuck were you shooting at our guys, if you saw nothing? Just for the fun of it?"

He hitched a shoulder and looked away.

"What about the Fury? How long have you been with them?"

His smile turned cocky. "How long have you been circle jerking with those guys out there? You guys are the biggest bunch of pussies on the planet, kissing each other's asses."

So he was going to play it like that.

Taking my piece from the back of my jeans, I reached out, grabbed him by the shirt, and brought my gun to his face. "Listen to me. Don't be smart, whoever you are. If it was up to me and most of those guys out there, you'd be dead. So you should start being a little grateful you're still breathing air."

I felt him stiffen against me, and he started to sniffle again. "Fine," he said quietly, looking away.

I dropped him back on the chair and slid my piece back in my jeans. "Now. Like I said. Let's just have a conversation. What's your name?"

He looked away. "Yuran."

"Yuran?" I was already pretty sure the kid was yanking my chain again.

"Yeah. Yuran Asshole," he said, giving me a big smirk.

I backed up, brought the gun out again. I aimed it at his forehead. "I don't think you're understanding how close you are to dead?"

He shrugged, meeting my hard gaze with defiance. "Go on. Shoot me. I don't care."

"You don't?" I pressed the gun against his forehead so hard that he stiffened. I cocked the trigger. "All right, then . . ."

I wasn't going to do it. But I had a feeling about this kid.

And my feeling was right. He cracked, right down the middle.

He took a deep breath and started to shake. So he thought I was bluffing. "Wait. Wait," he said. "Okay. My name is Joel—er, J-Dawg. That's what the brothers call me."

I put the gun down again. Held out my hand. "Joel." I sure as hell wasn't going to call him by the name the Fury had christened him with. "That's more like it. I'm Hart."

He stared at my outstretched hand for a moment, then shook it warily, his eyes scanning me. "You're a Cobra."

I nodded. Proud. "I'm the secretary of the Steel Cobras. And you . . . you're a Fury prospect. Tell me about them. How long have you been with them?"

He rubbed at his nose. "Not long. Few months."

"Why? How'd you get involved with them?"

"Couple of buddies said they're the toughest guys in town. So I thought I should give them a look. And I liked what I saw," he said.

"And what did you see?"

One corner of his mouth quirked up. "Thought you'd like to know that."

"So you've heard of the Cobras?"

He nodded. "Yeah. I've heard of who you are. Also heard you were a bunch of pussies."

How anyone could admire the Fury was beyond me, but they'd undoubtedly been feeding their prospects all kinds of shit about us. "You think we're pussies? How long you been riding a bike? You looked like a goddamn six-year-old with training wheels out there."

He gave me a wounded look and his shoulders slumped. "Yeah. Got the bike a couple of weeks ago. But I'm getting there."

I remembered my first bike when I was fourteen. I didn't know much of anything back then, either. And didn't have anyone in the family to show me. Luckily, some of the Cobras at the garage had shown pity on me and pitched in to teach me all I needed to know. I chuckled.

"All right. Here's what we're going to do. I'm gonna take you out of here, to my apartment. You're going to do everything I say, and if you do, we let you live. If you don't, you die. Simple as that. You got it?"

He gave me a surly look, but then sighed. "Fine. Whatever."

I bent down to have a look at his eyes, under that unruly mop of hair. "Yeah?"

His voice got defensive and he sulked more. "I *said* yeah."

I leaned in real close to his face. "I don't think you do. The last thing you want in this world is the Cobras on your ass. Do you understand me? We'll be good to you. But if you fuck this up and go running back to the Fury, you won't just be Public Enemy Number One to us. We'll go after your whole goddamn family. Do you understand me?"

Not that we ever had, but this kid didn't know that. It had the desired effect. His eyes widened. He began to bob his head. "Yeah. Yeah, I understand."

"Good." I motioned to him, then went to get my helmet and keys. "Come on. Let's get out of here. It's fucking late. I'm beat."

EVIE MONROE

Chapter Two

Charlotte

"Aw, come on baby, what's wrong?" I said to a cute little fluffball as he grunted in his cage.

I opened the wire door and lifted the little black lop-eared bunny from his pile of timothy hay, scratching him behind his long ears. He'd been brought in with a GI infection, but now that had healed, and he was ready for adoption.

"Flopsy, you're doing good. The doc has given you the all clear. That means you can go find your fur-ever home!" I exclaimed, hearing him purr a little against my chest, his heartrate slowing.

Dr. Grace Andrews, the vet, smiled at me. "You have such a way with those shelter animals. That one wouldn't let anyone pick him up. He was so skittish."

I laughed. "This sweet baby? I can't believe it! He's nothing but a great big sweetheart."

She went back to her desk piled high with work. "That's what you say about all of our patients. I don't know what we would ever do without you, Charlotte."

I looked into the bunny's black button eye. What could I say? The rescues were my favorite of all the animals brought into the Aveline Bay Veterinary practice. I understood lost-and-lonely better than anyone. This particular one was all black with a little white spot on his nose. "He's so adorable."

"He's up for adoption!" Dr. Andrews reminded me.

I set him back in the cage with a reluctant sigh and started to scuff away in my comfy work shoes and scrubs. "Don't tempt me."

I was so on the verge, as I was at least once a day, at this job. The problem was, my tiny apartment was a two-pet establishment. And I was already testing that to the limit. I had two . . . dogs. But also, one practically hairless cat, a bunny, a blind turtle, and a gerbil with three legs. And my stupid brother.

I lived in constant worry that my landlord would find out and boot my ass. But I couldn't help it. I loved all the abandoned and sad creatures of the world.

Speaking of abandoned and sad . . .

I walked to the reception area and reached into my purse for my phone. I stared at the display with a rush of disappointment.

No messages.

Dejected, I pocketed the phone, then grabbed my jacket and hoisted my purse onto my shoulder. I said goodbye to the rest of the techs in the reception area of the veterinary hospital and walked out to the parking lot, cursing the name of my little brother.

We'd talked about this Jojo knew better. Knew how I worried. And yet he just seemed to get worse and worse. At nineteen, now, I thought after he graduated from high school, he'd get a job, start taking on more responsibility and help out around the house. I didn't know he'd turn into a big old party-loving loser who hardly ever came home.

When I slid into the driver's seat of my car, I checked his Instagram to see if he'd posted anything. He loved posting himself doing keg-stands or getting high.

But nope. He hadn't updated his status in a week.

I tried to tell myself that it was all normal teen behavior, and I should be happy he was having a normal teen life, since I'd been all about working at the grocery store at night, and college during the day when I was his age. No time for fun. He had it easy.

He could have at least sent me a text to let me know he was alive. Was that asking too much?

I turned the key in the ignition and tried not to worry. But he was still just a kid in so many ways. And he hadn't come home last night, or the night before.

Usually, when he stayed out drinking with his friends, he'd let me know he was okay. Send a quick text so I'd know where he was. So I wouldn't worry.

Not this time.

Of course, he was notoriously bad about remembering to charge his phone. Maybe his battery just died.

Or maybe . . .

I swallowed, once again thinking the thoughts that had consumed my mind during my entire shift. *He's getting worse, Charlotte, and you know it. It's got to be those loser friends of his. Maybe he's gone from pot to something worse.*

Pulling out of the parking lot, I tried to rein in my brain to stop it from imagining the worst—Jojo dead of an overdose in someone's basement, or in a ditch from a drunk driving accident. Considering the pictures I'd seen on his Instagram lately, neither of those scenarios was much of a stretch.

I turned up the music loud as I drove across the town of Aveline Bay, to the apartment we shared. I was twenty-five, now, six years older than my baby brother, but in my head, I'd always be his mom.

His dad, too.

Pretty much his everything.

Growing up, we'd never had much in the way of parental figures. I was seven when our parents drove away and left us at the Circle K, too strung out on heroin to realize we weren't in the car with them. Joel could barely walk at the time, a little over a year old and an adorable little bouncing boy.

I still remember sitting in the police headquarters that night, thinking they'd arrested me for being a bad girl and afraid I'd spend the rest of my life in jail. They'd taken Jojo away from me, and I sat on one of those hard plastic chairs in the waiting room, in my pink unicorn shirt and pigtails, while everyone buzzed around, ignoring me.

Eventually, a social worker named Ms. Nettles came in and told me that my parents had gone away for a while, and that I'd be living in a home with other children while they tried to find a more permanent place for me.

I screamed my head off. Not for my mom. Not for my dad. They'd always been transient in my life, floating in and out, often absent when I needed them.

I screamed for Jojo.

Whatever I did must have worked, because two days later, we were placed with a foster family, but together. I still remember holding his sweaty hand in mine. He looked up at me and said, "La-la?" his name for me, his dark coffee-colored eyes full of sadness and confusion.

That placement didn't last, though.

After that, we bounced around from foster family to foster family. Sometimes we'd be placed together, sometimes not.

Whenever not, I was miserable. I acted out. I screamed. I cried. I made them know that I was not happy with the arrangement until I went back into the "foster kid shuffle," as I'd come to call it.

So the second I turned eighteen and went out on my own, I applied to be Jojo's legal guardian.

Forever, it'd been just the two of us, against the world.

I struggled a lot figuring out when I should be a parent and when I should just be his sister. Especially when he technically became an adult. We'd been fighting more and more about that. He kept saying he didn't need me telling him what to do anymore. Kept threatening to move out.

Maybe I should have let him. Allow him to make his own mistakes.

But yet, I couldn't.

I was everything to him—and he was pretty much all I had, as well.

So for the past few weeks, I'd been bending over backward for him. I didn't hound him about getting a new job after Jack in the Box fired him. I'd let him get that awful, death trap of a used motorcycle with most of his savings, instead of insisting he help me make rent. I hadn't said a word when I saw him hanging out with these tough leather-bound guys in front of the liquor store. I'd let a lot of bad stuff slide.

Maybe I shouldn't have.

God, if this was the way parents felt about their decisions—all this regret and self-doubt—I never wanted to be a mother.

I pulled into our shitty apartment complex and looked up at number 313, our little slum on the third floor.

Our one large, picture window looked into the living room. Seeing it dark, my stomach sank.

I sat there, my hands on the steering wheel, wondering where he'd be if not here. Oh, I could think of thousands of places in Aveline Bay, all of them bad.

I'd gotten sick of him last night. I'd found ants in our living room from the dirty dishes he left all over the place, so I'd had it. I stormed through the apartment on a cleaning binge, the animals all staring at me, a woman possessed. He usually locked his door, but I could smell the stench of his body odor and old food from the hallway, so I found a hammer and broke in.

That's when I found it.

He had a gun.

Just lying there on his dresser, innocent as a hairbrush.

I had no idea where he'd gotten it from, or that he even knew how to use one. I'd plucked it up from his dresser like it was a live, dangerous thing and held it out in front of me like a grenade that was about to go off.

When he'd gotten back, I'd started to lay into him about it, but he took one look at his open door and screamed at me, "What the fuck? What gives you the right to go through my things?"

I'd never seen him so angry.

Then he called me a fucking bitch.

Sure, he'd used those words before. What teenage kid didn't? But he'd never, ever used them on me. As much as we argued, I always felt like he knew I was his best ally. His "La-La." We had a certain respect for each other because of our shared history. Our relationship was sacred. Or so I'd thought.

I'd just stared at him, stunned, as all the air left my lungs. Whatever complaints I'd had in my throat died instantly.

He'd grabbed the gun easily, like he'd been handling one his entire life. He shoved it into the pocket of his jacket, and stormed out, his dark hair in his face, black eyes never meeting mine. Maybe he was strung out. A second later, I heard him speeding away on that stupid motorcycle.

That was the last time I saw him. Almost twenty-four hours ago.

Bracing myself for disappointment, I cut the engine and climbed the two flights of stairs to my place. Sometimes, when he'd hear my key in the lock, Jojo'd run to greet me, open the door for me before I could twist the key. I'd go into a warm apartment and a macaroni and cheese dinner he'd cooked for me.

He hadn't done that for me in a while.

This time, I opened the door to a dark apartment.

When I went inside, all the animals raced to see me—Burt and Ernie, Opie, and the little bunny. But other than that, sure enough, everything was just as when I'd left for work.

Jojo hadn't been home.

Chapter Three

Hart

On the way back to my apartment, I would've stopped at one of the 24-hour fast food places that lined the main drag near my place, especially since I didn't have much in my fridge, but I didn't want anyone— especially the Fury—to see me with the kid. I'd had him turn his prospect kutte inside out before he got on the back of my bike, just in case.

I parked outside my apartment and we went upstairs, opened the door, and I threw my shit down in the hallway. The kid looked around at all the extra computer parts and peripherals I had scattered all over the place in cardboard boxes. He squinted at my coffee table, where I'd been building a robotic arm. I expected him to make a smart remark about it being a shithole, but he didn't. He just yawned.

I'd been thinking about where I'd keep him on the drive over. If I let him sleep on the couch, I couldn't trust him not to escape the second I went into the bedroom. The only option was letting him have my bed. And that thought pissed me off, but I muttered, "You can have the bed," before going into the kitchen and grabbing a couple of beers. I peered inside the fridge.

"You hungry? I got grilled cheese and . . . cheese. And bread."

He shrugged and made himself comfortable on a kitchen island stool. "Whatever."

I pulled out enough bread and cheese for two. I started the grill, popped the top on the beer, and slid one over to him. "So . . . you said your friends got you interested in the Fury?"

He crossed his arms, the tough guy again. "That ain't none of your bees wax."

"Look, kid. We can sit here in absolute fucking silence and look at each other while we eat, but I think it'd be better if we got to know each other," I said, getting the sandwiches ready for the grill. "Me? I joined the Cobras when I was fourteen. Unofficially, of course.

Couldn't really join until I got my motorcycle license. So, I was a prospect at sixteen. How old are you?"

He stared at me, then reached over, grabbed the beer, and took a swig, like *Fuck you, you just gave an underage kid beer.* Not that it mattered to me; my dad had given me my first beer at six. "Nineteen."

I raised an eyebrow. He looked younger to me. "Why you want to join a club?"

He just stared at me. I kept talking. "My dad ran the garage where all the Cobras went." I flipped the sandwiches and shrugged. "I was the nerd, the fat kid with the brains who always had his head in a computer. Head of the robotics club at school. I was bullied like crazy at school. My father didn't like me hanging around the garage, but when I did, I would talk with the guys from the club and they were all so badass. No one ever fucked with them. I wanted to be one of them."

He didn't say anything for a long time. He just sat there, flipping the cap from the beer bottle. Then, he let out an incredulous laugh and said, "*You* were a nerd?"

That was a good sign, from a kid who'd called the Cobras a bunch of pussies and fags. "Yeah. Big-time. Still kind of am. I like to tinker on shit like my father." I held up my hands, which were covered in cuts and calluses. "See?"

He motioned over to the robotic arm on the coffee table. "What's that?"

"That? I'm always building shit to help at the Leaf. That's a robotic arm that's going to be part of a drone for oil changes. My dad hated anything tech. But when I was sixteen, I gave him a diagnostic probe that could scan a car and give you a diagnosis in thirty seconds. Now, he's always having me make all this shit for him."

I left out the part about my father being a lifetime alcoholic, which was the real reason I'd made all that shit for him. Most of the time, the tremors were so bad he could barely hold a wrench anymore. And why I preferred tinkering up in my room instead of at the garage. My dad usually beat the shit out of me whenever I was in his path, so I tried to stay out of it.

The kid kept squinting at me. "Shit. Why are you not working for Microsoft or Apple or some shit like that?"

I shrugged. "Big corporations suck. And I like my life. The Cobras are my brothers. I got everything I need right here."

He gave me a doubtful look. He watched me in silence as I plated the grilled cheeses and slid one over to him. I turned off the stove and sat across from him. "So . . . what about you? You got parents?"

He shook his head.

I raised an eyebrow as I chewed my sandwich. "You on your own? Who do you live with?"

"My sister," he mumbled as he swallowed loudly. "But she don't want me around. I fucked her over too much. She got sick of me after I got fired from my job at Jack in the Box."

This was progress. He was actually saying more to me than half-form sentences and grunts. "She kicked you out?"

"Not really, but she probably will now, after what I did. But I'm not sure I want to go back."

"She's pissed at you just 'cause you got fired?"

He stuffed the rest of his sandwich in his mouth and chewed slowly, his Adam's apple bobbing in his throat. "No. Not just that. That was just the start of it. I got high in the bathroom so they canned me. I needed to make money because she's always short on rent and I'd been helping. I started dealing drugs around the high school. No big deal."

He was talking low, trying to be all tough, assert himself. I could still see the shadow of the scared boy underneath. The kid didn't have anywhere to go. He needed a friend. And if he really chose the Fury as his friends, he'd be fucked. I only hoped it wasn't too late.

"You use?"

He shrugged. "Little pot and stuff mostly. Other stuff sometimes."

"Don't know how the Fury is, but Cobras don't tolerate our guys doing drugs."

He gave me a defiant look. "They never said nothin' about that to me."

"So...what? Your sister found out about you dealing drugs?"

He shook his head. "No. Not Char. She works too much to notice much of anything I do. I was doing pretty well ..." He mumbled into his lap. "Then one of the Fury guys saw me on the street and told me I should join the club. That way, if the police came after me, I wouldn't be alone. He said it was like an extra level of protection 'cause no one fucks with them. I met with the guys and liked them. I never really had . . . anything like that, you know?"

"Yeah. I get it." As the bullied kid, I knew what having an MC on your side could do. But the Fury? I'd heard stories about them. They used their prospects as human shields. As far as I'd seen, and from what I'd heard from Zain, it wasn't a brotherhood. Not like the Cobras. "But how much do you know about the Fury?"

He let out a snort and gave me a sly look. "More than you."

I didn't know if that was true. In my years, I'd heard a lot. Yes, it was a lot of second-hand information, but I had first-hand information, too. In addition to Zain's horror stories, they'd kidnapped Nix's girl, nearly killed our president and his family, and the former president of the Fury had almost murdered his own daughter. And if that wasn't enough, the Fury had also bombed our first clubhouse and was fond of taking pot shots at us whenever they saw us around town.

I figured we had a pretty good reason to despise the hell out of them. But the Fury scum had probably filled this kid's head with a lot of lies about us. So telling him what I knew probably wouldn't have done a hell of a lot of good. It was their word against ours.

I backtracked. "So you ain't planning on going back to your sister?"

"Nah. She broke into my room though and found a gun I had, and who-knows-what else. She started yelling at me and telling me I needed to shape up. I've had it with her. I got on my bike and tore out of there. That was last night."

He'd cleaned his plate, so I took it from him and put both of ours in the sink. In my head, I wondered how hard it would be to get this sister to chain him up. Because right now, she was about the only friend he had.

"So where were you going to stay then?"

He shrugged.

"You new to Aveline Bay?" I asked him.

He shook his head.

That surprised me. "Because when you were out there, you were driving like you had no fucking clue where you were going."

He crossed his arms over a t-shirt for a band I'd never heard of. He had skinny arms with a little bit of muscle, like he'd recently been picking up the free weights. "I was supposed to meet someone from the Fury somewhere. But when I got there, nobody showed."

"Oh yeah? Who?"

"My sponsor."

"Who's your sponsor?"

He gnawed on the inside of his cheek. "Not sure I should be telling you all this. Why do you care?"

I shrugged. "I don't. Just making conversation."

That wasn't the only thing. I needed to get this guy to trust me and see if I could trust him. But right now, it felt like it was all up in the air.

Yeah, I saw a lot of myself in him. But that didn't mean I was going to let him out of my sight.

Not for one second.

Chapter Four

Charlotte

I paced around the little apartment, the sun fading to a dark night sky. I checked on the animals, filling their food and water and changing out litter, trying to decide what to do next.

I had to go past Jojo's bedroom to get to my bedroom at the end of the hallway. His door was open, just the way he'd left it when he stormed out the previous day.

I stopped in front of it, then peeked inside. I flipped on a light and scanned around. The gun had shocked me; now I wondered what other horrors I'd find.

It smelled awful, like feet and body odor and stale food. Dirty clothes almost completely covered the floor, and I saw a half-eaten Pop-Tart on top of the hamper.

If that was all I found, I'd be happy. But after finding that gun, I knew I'd find a lot worse.

I guessed he didn't have a permit. California had pretty steep gun laws. What would he do if the police stopped him? Did he care they could arrest him?

I moved around to one side of the bed, shuffling through an ankle-deep pile of dirty clothes. As I did, my toe smashed against something hard. I bent over, my mouth forming silent curses before screaming out a strangled "Gah!" of complete agony.

I lifted up a dirty Nirvana shirt and saw a dumbbell. That meant the rest of his weight set was probably around here, as well. This place was like a friggin' minefield.

I limped slowly, my toe aching like a mother and shoved aside some of the clothes on top of his messed up bed. I sat down onto the mattress, wondering if I should start calling police stations and hospitals.

Before my ass hit the sheets, I realized that they were gross with dirty stains. Ugh, I thought. When was the last time he'd washed these?

I stripped the bed and threw the sheets in the hamper. Then I sank down onto the bare mattress, looked around and wondered what other dangers lurked in here.

As I sat there, I thought of the times Jojo would come home from school and wrap his hands around my neck. He'd been such a little stinker, but also the biggest sweetheart, too. He'd made of his finger paintings and drawings in school for me. In middle school for a mother-son baseball game at school, he addressed the invitation to me, and we'd had a blast. At fifteen, I taught him to drive for the first time. Nervous, because he didn't want to screw up, he drove donuts around the high school parking lot at a top speed of fifteen miles per hour.

It didn't matter that he was only six years younger than me, or how old he got, or even that I was still his sister. And he was still my little brother. I loved him, no matter what.

I needed to find one of his friends to contact.

The problem was, I didn't know any of them. I only saw pictures of him partying with them in his social media posts. I didn't have phone numbers.

I started to rummage around some more, finding things I wish I hadn't. Condoms—well, he was nineteen, not nine, so I'd figured that was happening. A few dime bags with a little bit of pot residue in them. I'd learned about the pot smoking when his job kicked him to the curb, but I'd suspected that wasn't his first rodeo and he'd been a user long before then. A hardcore porn magazine—Blech.

Then I noticed something on the night table, under a couple of empty Coke cans. Something he'd drawn on the back of a napkin, a little doodle. Jojo could have a career as a great artist if he'd focus—he used to scribble cartoon characters all over his school notebooks.

He'd sketched a picture of a motorcycle silhouetted in flames, drawn, Hells Fury Forever. Underneath that in fancy letters it said, "J-DAWG".

J-Dawg? My little brother? What kind of stupid name was J-Dawg? Sure, he was a little misguided sometimes, but he wasn't a common thug.

At least, I hoped not.

I wanted to crumple it up. When he got the bike I thought he might get involved in a club. But whoever the Hells Fury guys were, I'd bet money I didn't have they were behind Jojo acting less like the Jojo I knew, and more like an America's Most Wanted poster boy.

I piled up some of his dirty clothes and threw them in the hamper along with his sheets, then carried an armful of dirty plates and glasses out to the kitchen. I tossed it all in the sink and sat down on the couch with my dogs, Burt and Ernie, and my kitty, Opie. Absently petting them, I looked up the number for the Aveline Bay Regional Hospital.

When someone answered, I said, "Hello, my brother is missing, and I'm worried about him. Could you tell me if you've admitted a Joel Grayson?"

"One moment." I put my feet up on the coffee table as I waited. "I'm sorry. No one by that name."

"Okay," I said, both relieved and frustrated. "Thank you."

I hung up and thought about calling the Aveline Bay police, but then a better idea came to me. I had a profile on Facebook, and one on Instagram, for the sole reason of checking up on Jojo's antics. He probably had some friends on there I could message.

I opened it up and realized he hadn't updated his Facebook page in over a year.

It was a long shot. But it was better than nothing. I opened up a few profiles of the people he'd been close to before and sent out a few messages. One of them replied right away: *Joel? No, haven't seen him in months. I thought he died.*

I threw back my head and rubbed my eyes. That was not what I wanted to hear. The way my parents had been when we were younger, I was super-sensitive to drugs and addiction.

So I did the only thing I could do. I went back to checking hospitals and police stations in the small towns and communities near Aveline Bay. Each time a nurse or officer put me on hold to check, I held my breath, waiting for the bad news.

It never came. None of the other hospitals or police departments had seen him, either.

The good news still didn't set my mind at ease.

Jojo wouldn't do this to me. But I had no idea what this "J-Dawg" Grayson would do.

EVIE MONROE

Chapter Five

Hart

By the time we got around to turning in, it was after three. I showed the kid to the bathroom and let him have free reign over my bedroom, knowing the most damage he could do was to the sheets. The bedroom had no windows he could escape out of, so I figured it was safe.

I stripped to my boxer briefs and stretched out on my lumpy couch with my robotic arm for company, staring at the ceiling.

As tired as I was, I couldn't sleep. Didn't want to risk the kid sneaking out on me while I was catching some Zs. I could have probably rigged up an alarm but didn't have the energy to do it.

Before I knew it, the sun peeked through the blinds and I hadn't dropped off for a second. Giving up on sleep, I got up and pulled on my jeans.

I pulled my phone out of my jacket and found the kid's there, too. I texted Cullen, *Cobras owe me big time for this shit.*

I scrubbed my hand through my hair and tried to take a look at the kid's phone. He had it password protected, but that wasn't a problem for me. I easily opened it and saw he had four percent of his battery left.

At my desk, I sorted through a bunch of geeky supplies and found what I needed to pry open the back of it. I added our own little tracking device, then went inside the programming guts and added the code that would allow us to listen in on all the conversations that the kid had from this phone. By then, I'd used up the battery.

I set it down on the coffee table, went to the kitchen, and poured myself a bowl of cereal. As I sat there eating, I got a text back from Cullen: *Good man, senator.*

Yeah, whatever. I thought of Jet, probably getting some pussy with that hot doctor of his right now, and I didn't even get to sleep in my own bed. Where was the justice in that? Apparently, it paid to be an asshole.

An hour later, the kid still hadn't woken up. Fucking sleeping beauty. I had to go into my bedroom and bang on the wall. "Hey. Kid."

Nothing.

"Joel." I banged harder.

Nothing.

What the . . .?

I stalked across the room and shoved him. He groaned.

I opened my dresser and pulled on a t-shirt. As I turned around, he snored again, back asleep.

I reached over and yanked the sheet off the bed. "Get your ass up."

He rolled over and cracked open an eye. "What time is it?"

"Late. Come on. Get your ass up. I want to talk to you."

He sat up in bed and rubbed his eyes. He had a skeletal, concave chest and already sported a tattoo on his arm. Something with a skull. Tough guy. "Fuck," he moaned. "I want to sleep."

I motioned to the bathroom. "Wash up. Take a shower. Then meet me out in the living room."

I strode out to the couch and peeled off the sheet and covers I'd used. Fifteen minutes later, the kid appeared. He looked even more run-down than yesterday and hadn't taken a shower. I could smell him from across the room.

He sat down at the same seat he'd occupied last night at the kitchen island, and I pushed a bowl and a box of cereal over to him, then got him the milk from the fridge.

As he poured it, he looked at me warily. "What did you want to talk about?"

I leaned over the island. "Listen, dude. I can't keep you here. But I need to know what it is you think you saw last night. So you've got to level with me."

He shoveled a spoonful of cereal into his mouth and said, "Honest. Nothing. I saw two guys with Cobras on their kuttes, and I dunno. I thought if I offed one of them, it would impress the Fury."

I stared him down, until his tough-guy façade started to crumble. His shoulders slumped. "I know, I know. That was damn stupid. If I killed someone, I'd go to prison forever and Char would never forgive me."

"Char? Your sister?" I asked.

"Yeah." He mumbled.

"Sounds like she's got a real short leash on you."

He laughed bitterly. "Yeah, I guess she does. She's had to be protective of me 'cause we grew up in foster care. She's always been too serious for me. She wouldn't know fun if it bit her on the ass." He shook his head. "I wouldn't have been able to hit your guy, anyway."

"What were you doing down there?"

He shrugged. "I don't know. Scar sent me."

Scar. The name rang a bell, but I couldn't place it. "Scar?"

"He's the vice president."

Oh, right. The vice president who'd assumed the position after Cullen had killed Bruiser. "Why did he send you?"

He shrugged again. I began to think he used the gesture in place of speech. "Why else? To see what you guys were doing."

I scratched at the three-day stubble on my chin that was on its way to becoming a beard. "You do that a lot?"

He dunked some of the cereal with his spoon and bobbed his head. "You kidding me? I've been following you for the past week."

I had to laugh. Was he serious? He was about as graceful on a bike as a bull in a china shop. How had we not noticed him? From the look on his face, he wasn't exaggerating.

Christ, we were getting sloppy. "What else have you done, gangster?"

"Well, Slade's a little bit all over the place with what he wants done. I get the feeling he's kind of nuts. But one thing he was pretty set on was tracking you guys 24/7."

I stared at him. This was good info. He was still referring to Slade as if he was alive. Maybe he didn't have any idea what Nix and Jet were doing that night. If so, he couldn't have been following us that closely. Or he was just fucking stupid.

From what Joel was saying, if they were so interested in our operations, it was clear we were ruffling their feathers. "So what do they know about us?"

Joel shrugged. "Everything."

That wasn't good. "What do you mean, everything?"

"All of it. They know your business of boosting cars. They know who your contacts are. They want to bring you down, but they're searching for the right time to do it. They said you killed a couple of their guys in a shootout a few months back. Fury is gonna fuck you guys up."

"They kidnapped an innocent girl," I muttered.

"They said she wasn't innocent."

I rolled my eyes. Of course they did. "Look, believe what you want. But Cobras ain't in the business of hurting innocent people to get ahead in our operations. That's what started this war in the first place. The Fury nearly killed a woman, and we don't look too kindly on that. And that's the truth."

He stared at me for a long time. "Yeah. Well, some things about them make me wonder . . ."

Cracks in his alliance with the Hell's Fury? I pounced on it. "Like what?"

"Like I said, Slade can be one mean son of a bitch. He's done some things that scared the crap out of me. The first day I went to their clubhouse, I made the mistake of trying to talk to his daughter. The guys told me that if Slade found out, I'd never walk again."

Sounded familiar. I knew Slade's daughter, Cait, because she was now Drake's girl. The things he went through to be with her? Slade was the one who ended up dead, but it very easily could've been Drake. "I don't doubt it."

"And there's other fucked up stuff. Rituals and hazing they make the prospects go through. I don't like that shit. It's all a bunch of bullshit so the patched members can flex their muscles and look like hot shit." He gave me a curious look. "Do the Cobras do stuff like that?"

I shook my head. "Nah. What the fuck for? Sounds like stupid college shit."

He nodded and said softly, "That's good, man. Really good."

Maybe he hadn't made the decision to jump ship and join us. But at least he was being honest with me right now. I wasn't one-hundred-percent sure he wasn't feeding me a line of bull so I'd let him go, but he seemed sincere.

As he finished up his cereal, I said, "So what are you going to do when you get out of here?" I was testing him.

He raised an eyebrow. "When?"

"Whenever. You think I'm going to keep you here forever?"

He smiled the first real smile I'd seen since I met him. "I've been thinking about my sister. She doesn't deserve me giving her shit. I called her a bitch, and that was a big mistake. I've got to talk to—"

He stopped suddenly, and his eyes widened. He felt around his pockets and cursed.

"What's up?"

He looked around wildly. "Shit! I need to call her! Where's my phone? She's probably out of her mind right now, worrying about me."

I went to the coffee table and lifted up the black screen. "It's dead, though."

"Oh, fuck. Oh, shit," he said, his voice frantic. He vised his head in his hands, stooped over. Jesus, this sister of his must've had fangs. "Can I borrow your phone?"

I shook my head. I'd heard too many stories of people borrowing phones and fucking with them, so I never let anyone borrow my phone. I had a charger for that model but I didn't let on.

"Look, I'll do you one better. Let's go back to the garage and pick up your bike. I bet my guys have fixed it by now. And then I'll follow you over to your place. Okay?"

He frowned. "You guys have my bike?"

I nodded. "Yeah. We weren't just gonna let it stay by the side of the road. We took it back to the garage, and I bet it's better than it was before you crashed it."

"Okay. Cool." He nodded slowly, then grabbed his phone from me and shoved it into the pocket of his jeans. "Yeah. Let's go."

Chapter Six

Charlotte

The neighbors downstairs must have hated me. I paced around the house, stomping heavy-footed, ready to blow a gasket.

Where the fuck is he?

I'd always thought he was the person who knew me best on this planet. He had to know I was frantic, by now. So that meant that the person I cared the most about in this world didn't give a fuck about how I felt.

And God, it stung.

As I stormed about the apartment like a tornado, the animals followed me. Burt and Ernie paced behind me, constantly getting caught up between my legs. Opie just watched from the sofa, eyes going back and forth like a pendulum, like she was too classy to engage in such an activity.

Then I lifted my phone and dialed again, and it went straight to voicemail.

If I had a dollar for every time I called Jojo only to have the phone go right to voicemail, I'd be rich. He never remembered to charge his phone. But if his phone was dead, he'd find another way to get through to me. Always. And this was going on a full day. He'd never ignored me for this long.

I went to the sink and opened the medicine cabinet. Brought down his prescription of Theophylline and opened it. We got it on a monthly basis, and the month was almost over, so he should have had only a pill or two left. But there were twelve in there.

That wasn't good. He needed to take those pills every day, like clockwork, to control his asthma. He'd been taking them since he was twelve. He knew this.

When I got my hands on him, I'd rip him a new one, the dumb shit. But I couldn't think about that now. I needed to find him.

Maybe he'd wanted to get in touch with me. Maybe he was dead, or dying, or crying out for help.

After a few more minutes of pacing, I threw myself down at the couch and let out a "FUCK!" The pressure was just too much.

As I was sitting there, hunched over with my head in my hands, I heard it.

A motorcycle.

Actually, two of them.

At first, I thought I was hearing things, or that the bikes belonged to someone else. But Jojo's little jalopy sounded unlike any other bike out there—metallic and raspy, like it was puttering toward a certain death. Then it got closer, until the whole building vibrated and the noise appeared to be coming from right under the window.

I jumped to my feet and ran to the front of the apartment, just as the noise cut out. I tilted the blinds for a look. Sure enough, there was Jojo, climbing off his bike, next to another rider twice his size. Jojo stood there, flexing his nonexistent muscles, trying to look cool and relaxed for the big douche with him, both of them taking off their helmets.

I ripped opened the door and flew down the stairs, into the parking lot. I didn't care about the other prick. All I saw right then was Jojo. And as happy as I was to see him alive and kicking, I also wanted to kill him for putting me through this crap for the last day.

I approached him as he was tucking his helmet under his arm. I took his face in my hands, looking for any sign of injury, and he shirked away, turning on his cool act. "Are you okay?" I demanded.

He shook his head. "Yeah, I'm fine. I—"

As he started to step onto the curb, I shoved into his chest, full force, with both hands. "Then why didn't you fucking call me, you asshole?"

He staggered back. Lightweight. I'd dealt with people a hell of a lot bigger than him.

"Whoa, what—" he started to say.

"Don't you whoa me!" I shouted at him, my face hot and my fists curled. I pushed him again. "What the fuck do you think you're doing?"

"I'm sorry!" His voice cracked and he held up his hands in surrender, and those chocolate brown eyes got all puppy-dog on me. I refused to give in.

"I—"

"You're not sorry! If you were sorry, you would've done me the courtesy of a fucking phone call!" I shouted, shoving him again.

This time, he crossed his arms defensively over his chest, standing taller. "Give me a break. My phone's dead."

"And you couldn't borrow someone else's? Where the fuck were you?" I insisted, stalking away with my hands on my hips. I took a deep breath, trying to calm myself. As I faced away from him, I noticed a couple apartment doors opening, and people looking outside to check on the commotion.

I was beyond caring. And those deep breaths? They did nothing for me. I was still pissed beyond belief.

"You know I thought you were dead? I was imagining you lying dead in a ditch and thinking I'd get a phone call saying I needed to identify your body. You know I—"

I stopped suddenly when I heard something.

Laughter.

Not happy laughter, but laughter like, *Who is this crazy, overreacting bitch?*

Okay. I'd already lost my shit by this time. But if anything could've made me lose my shit and smear it all over the place in a fucking finger-painting, it was this prick, laughing at me. I didn't care how tough or cool he was. I'd fucking eat him for breakfast.

I turned to my little brother's companion. In contrast to my brother, he was not little. He had bare, tanned arms, big and thick, and a tattoo on his bicep peeking out. His face was covered in a cinnamon-colored stubble, and his long reddish blond hair was pulled back in a ponytail. I think his look was exactly what my brother was trying to achieve, in his dirty jeans and leather vest. Tall, broad, and leaning against his bike like he was auditioning me for a job, this guy regarded me like I was the funniest joke he'd ever heard.

Oh, hell to the fucking no. I narrowed my eyes at him. "And who the fuck do you think you are? Some Son of Anarchy? Badass biker? Wannabe?"

The guy stared back at me for a few seconds, not saying anything. As I looked at him, my face started to heat up. Because he wasn't just one of those fuck-it-all badasses who scared most people enough to make them pee their pants.

He was actually kind of . . . *hot*. Really hot. He had these deep hazel, tiger eyes, green with flecks of light that settled on me and wouldn't let go. He tight, army green t-shirt hugged his body so tight I could see the rise of his pecs. His mouth lifted but only on one side, in a surly, full of attitude smile, baring one dimple.

I'd never had a guy look at me like that before. Amused, scrutinizing, assessing me but . . . also mentally undressing me at the same time.

I felt naked and also kind of, head-to-toe buzzy, like I'd said something wrong.

Shit, what had we been talking about? My mind had gone completely blank, all as a result of those feral eyes of his.

Little by little, it flooded back. I bit my tongue as I realized what I'd called him. I started to backtrack as he crossed his arms in front of him. "Sons of Anarchy, huh? You watch the show?"

Fine. If I couldn't take it back, I might as well press forward. Didn't matter how hot he was. I was in the right here, and my brother was clearly in the wrong, the result of listening to scumbags like this one. "Are you the one responsible for my little brother looking like a stupid thug and not treating me with any respect?"

He didn't say anything. Just laughed some more, then licked his lips. Those bright hazel eyes were, unmistakably, on my lips. What was it he found so fascinating about them? Was it because I was the first person who'd ever stood up to him and all those muscles of his?

Well, they didn't intimidate me. There was plenty more where that came from.

I snarled at him, "What the hell is so funny?"

Finally, he did speak. He opened his mouth and said one word, in a low, grumbling voice. "You."

That was it. I saw red. I thought about shoving him but he was so big, so manly and muscular . . . so blatantly sexual, I didn't want to get closer. I scowled at him. "Kindly stay the fuck out of our business."

I turned to Jojo and got ready to unload on him some more.

But the big guy just laughed some more. I looked over, and now that surly, one-sided smile was big and baring a set of perfectly white teeth. He threw his head back with laughter, as if I was the funniest thing on earth.

"Are you fucking kidding me right now?" I said to him. "Go away. This is family business."

"Er—" Jojo suddenly broke in. "Char . . ."

I wagged a finger in his face. "You shut up. You go upstairs and you're cleaning your room for the rest of the day. I don't even want to see your face right now. Do you hear me?"

He cringed. So he didn't like being treated like a kid in front of his big, strong new BFF, was that it? Well, fuck that. He should have been glad I wasn't talking about how his dirty underwear never made it into the hamper or the fact that his sheets were more come-stains than cotton because of his never-ending jacking off.

Jojo hung his head and started down the path to the apartment.

Good. I lifted my chin to face Mr. Incredible Eyes. I set my jaw and took the time to choose my words. "Who the fuck do you think you are?"

He opened his mouth to speak, but I didn't want to hear it. I held up my palm. I had to say my piece.

"Wait. Don't tell me. I don't want to know. Just know that Jojo was once a really good kid. And ever since he's been hanging out with the likes of you, he's changed. And I don't like it. He doesn't have parents, and he hasn't had the easiest time with staying on the straight and narrow. He doesn't need you filling his head with ideas that he can be a gangster and go shooting people. So I'd prefer if you found some other impressionable kid to sink your claws into. Do you understand me?"

I took a desperately needed breath after I finished that speech. I waited for a response.

He didn't give one. He just kept staring, undoing me bit by bit with the light in those eyes of his.

By the time he did open his mouth, I was practically salivating for his answer. But it wasn't a yes, or a no, or even a fuck off, like I expected.

He simply said, "Hart."

My brow creased in confusion. "What?"

"You asked me who the fuck I thought I was," he said, extending his hand out to me to shake. "The name is Hart. And I ain't any son of anarchy. I'm anarchy itself."

Chapter Seven

Hart

So, Jojo had a little spitfire of a sister.

Not to mention, she was damn sweet. She wore an old, open, grungy flannel shirt that must've been a boyfriend's. She wore her dark hair in a ponytail, had dark eyes like her brother, and her short shorts and a tight camisole that showed me the outline of her nipples turned me on. To top it all off, her, her taut stomach sported a little belly ring.

Fuck, I wanted to suck on that belly ring. Lick all of her, from head to toe. Where the fuck did she get hips like that, that tight waist, those tits . . .?

Holy fuck, she was hot.

I held my hand out, waiting for her to shake it. Introduce herself. But I didn't just want that. I wanted to touch her. All over. But her hand would be a good start.

She didn't bite. She tossed her ponytail over her shoulder and said, "I don't care who you are. Stay away from my little brother."

I pulled my hand away. "If that's what you want. But the kid is nineteen. You can't stop him from doing what he wants."

Her lips puckered and she snarled, "Oh yeah? That's what you think. He'll listen to me because he doesn't want my foot up his ass."

Behind her, Joel waited at the steps to the apartment complex, watching us. I glanced back at this sweet little girl in front of me with the red face. She blew some rebellious strands of dark hair off her forehead and exhaled heavily, fisting her hands like she was ready to fight. Like she was daring me to touch her little brother.

She really thought she was something tough, didn't she? I guessed that was where her brother got it from.

The girl was half my size. I probably had seventy-five pounds on her. I couldn't help it.

I started to laugh again.

Her eyes brimmed with fire. "What's so fucking funny?"

She was. God, she was cute all riled up like that. I hadn't laughed this hard in a long time. I shook my head and raised my palms up to her. "Nothing. Nothing. I was just seeing your brother home. That's all."

She lowered her fists a little. "That's all? Then where was he?"

"Well, he was getting himself into a little trouble last night. But I took care of it. He's good now. I've been watching him."

She pressed her lips together, and her eyes flitted down to my kutte. "You took care of it? You've been watching him?"

I nodded. She pointed at the Cobra patch on my kutte. "You have a different patch than Jojo has. What does that mean?"

"That's right. I'm from a different club."

She frowned. "How is that possible? I told him I didn't want him messing around with any of those gangs. The drugs, the violence, the . . . it's not his scene. It shouldn't be his scene." She shook her head. "What kind of trouble was he getting himself into?"

I gave her a smirk. "You seem to know all about us, with our drugs and violence. Use your imagination."

"Tell me," she demanded, coming up real close to me. She smelled fantastic. Like apples.

I leaned into scent her, drawing her in slowly.

"What are you . . ." Her face twisted, and the next thing I knew, she brought her foot down hard, on my boot. She was barefoot, and I had steel-reinforced toes. It didn't do much of anything. Even so, she ground her foot down on my toe, like she was trying to murder it. It felt like a mosquito, breathing on me.

I looked down. "What the fuck are you doing?"

She sucked her lips in, a determined look on her face. "Tell me!"

I just started to laugh again at the feisty, crazy little woman. As I threw my head back, the bitch kneed me in the balls.

I leaned forward, sputtering as I grabbed at my nuts. Fireworks exploded in my vision as the pain nearly took my breath away. "What the—"

"Tell me!"

I took a few deep breaths and managed to get control of myself. When I spoke, my voice was almost back to normal. "The usual shit guys like us get into and the reason you don't want him hanging out with a guy like me."

She sighed. "So can you be more specific, motorcycle man? Is it drugs?"

I could've told her that he'd been shooting a gun and leading the police on a chase through all of Aveline Bay. But I didn't want to worry her any more. For the kid's sake. If she found that out, I wouldn't put it past her to lock him up in a dungeon inside her apartment. "Nah. Just having some fun. Your brother said you don't know anything about that."

She considered this, then looked over her shoulder for her brother. "I know how to have fun. The things Jojo has been getting into have been borderline illegal, though. That's not fun to me. That's stupid. Being in a motorcycle club? Stupid."

I grinned at her. "Aw. Don't you like to live on the edge?"

"No," she said defiantly. "I've done that enough, growing up. I'm happy with what I do. And I want Jojo to be happy, too. He's a smart, good kid. I don't know why he thinks he needs to hang out with the likes of you."

"The likes of me?"

She nodded. "Yeah. You and your macho bullshit. Toting guns around, acting like hot shit. Your testosterone is showing. No one's impressed."

I started to laugh again but stifled it quickly because she was still close enough to deliver Armageddon two-point-oh on my balls.

I sucked in a breath and studied her for a minute. "All right. Well. Honestly? It's nothing. We're just acquaintances through the two clubs. We went out last night, had some fun, and his phone died."

She crossed her arms. "And you didn't let him use your phone because . . ."

I shrugged. "My phone died, too."

"Oh, what a terrible night for technology," she said sarcastically, lifting her chin. She looked back over at him and sighed. "I don't want to hear this happening to him again."

I gave her a nod and said, "Okay mama. I promise we won't do it again. We'll charge our phone fully before we go anywhere."

She tossed her ponytail, still in a huff. "No. Don't you get it? You're not going to see him again. If I hear about that, I swear, I'll rearrange your face."

She held up a tiny, pale fist that was about the size of a doll's. Then she whirled around and nearly collided face-first with her brother, who'd come out to see me.

"What are you—I said get inside!" she barked at him, pointing forcefully toward the apartment complex. How'd that tiny little thing get such a big voice?

"Yeah, but . . ." he looked at me. "You going?"

I guess he was wondering if he had permission to go. He might have been awkward, couldn't ride or shoot worth a fuck, but at least he was good at following directions. He had balls, too; doing what Scar had said without question, alone. Maybe he would make a good patched member one day.

I yawned. It didn't matter what I did, now. The tracker I'd put in his phone would check him and make sure he stayed in line. "Yeah. But listen."

His eyes snapped up to mine, ensuring I had his full attention. So the kid was learning.

"You can't let the Fury know we talked. If the Fury try to get in touch with you, or if you promised them you'd be there, just go along like everything's the same. We'll get together tonight, understand? I got your number from your phone before it died. Keep your phone charged. I text you, you come. Okay?"

He nodded, his head hanging.

"If you don't check in, kid, we'll find you."

He nodded, agreeing. My eyes flitted up to his sister, who was watching us, eyes slowly filling with rage. Not long before that dam burst.

I took it as my cue to leave.

I stepped off the curb and grabbed my helmet. Not fast enough. Suddenly she was in front of the bike. "What do you mean, get together tonight? I just told you! He's not seeing you at all! In my house it's my rules! You can go fuck yourself!"

I smiled down at her as I fastened on my helmet. I didn't say a word. I was already learning that my silent routine did something very interesting to her. It made her furious. Which made her look even hotter. She was shaking, out of control.

Luckily, my bike was between us, so my balls were protected.

She leaned forward and put her hands on my handlebars. "Would you speak?"

I straddled my bike. "All right," I said, settling in. "Get off my bike so I can leave, baby."

I put my hands on the handlebars, right next to hers, and rose up on my bike like I was going to jump on the kickstart. I thought that might've scared her away but not this girl. She met my eyes with defiance. "No. Not until you tell me you're going to leave Jojo alone."

Behind her, Joel called out, "Hey, Char—"

"Stay out of this, Jojo! You're in enough trouble already!" she snapped, not looking in his direction. To me, she said, "I don't want you texting him. I don't want him seeing you, ever again. Do you hear me?"

I gave her a smirk. "Well. Mama has spoken."

"Is that a yes?"

I mock-saluted her. "It's a yes ma'am."

She narrowed her eyes. "You promise?"

Holy shit, this girl was unbelievable. I had a feeling she'd be even more unbelievable, bouncing on my cock. "You want me to fucking pinky-swear?"

She stared at me for almost a full minute, before slowly getting off the front end of my bike.

I started my bike, and as it roared to life under me, she winced in disgust. She whirled and as I pulled out of the space, I could already see her wagging her finger threateningly at her little brother.

Wow, she was something else.

But it was a win for me. Unless, the Cobras were involved, I rarely kept my promises, anyway. And I might not have cared too much about the brother, but I sure as hell wanted to see Charlotte again.

EVIE MONROE

Chapter Eight

Charlotte

I was well aware that I didn't have the healthiest view of sex in the world.

I'd lost my virginity to one of my foster brothers when I was thirteen and he was eighteen. Then, I'd been raped by one of my foster fathers at the age of fifteen. We switched around from school to school, so I never fit in with anyone and was always the outcast. I never had an actual, normal boyfriend, who'd take me on dates and talk to me and treat me like a normal human being.

When I was eighteen and working at the grocery store to make ends meet so I could support Jojo and go to school, a few of the managers there indicated to me that I could make extra money by helping them out.

At first, I'd thought it was just stocking shelves overnight, but I soon learned they had something else in mind. I became pretty famous there, giving blow jobs to the male employees by the dumpsters for fifty dollars a pop. Once, I'd had sex with the produce manager for a hundred, and then he invited me to a party with his friends, where I was shared by all the men for a thousand dollars.

That gave me enough to pay the rent for two months. I felt rich. And by then, I had already lost any dignity I might have had. All I was focused on was survival, on creating the best life possible for Jojo and me.

And we survived.

After that, I got my Associates and then a friend of mine from school had a vet father who was looking for a new vet tech. The pay was amazing, compared to what I'd been making. I jumped on the job, and we've been living in the lap of luxury ever since.

Well, sort of. I didn't have to go through the bruised and broken bin at the supermarket to put together our dinner, and the days of blowjobs for money were long behind me.

Jojo didn't know about any of that. Maybe if he did, he wouldn't have treated me the way he did when I climbed the stairs to the apartment.

For one, he'd locked the goddamn door on me.

I banged on the door with my fist. Again, neighbors tilted their blinds to look at me.

When he opened the door, he avoided my eyes and just sauntered to the couch, plopped himself down, and picked up a bowl of cereal he'd poured himself.

I stalked to the center of the room in an I-mean-business kind of way. All the animals at my feet jumped to attention, but the asshole on the sofa just shoveled Cheerios into his mouth, staring like a zombie at the television set. Some football game.

"Hello?" I waved my hand in front of his face.

He blinked. "Yeah?" Okay, that was it. I was tired of his shit. I stalked over to the TV and turned it off.

"Hey!" he jumped up and reached for the remote, but I snatched it from the coffee table before he could.

"You really think you're going to come in here after being MIA without calling me ,and I'm just going to let it blow over?" I demanded, crossing my arms in front of me.

He raised an eyebrow at me in a kind of surly way that reminded me of the jerk I'd just met outside. "I was hoping."

"Well you hoped wrong, mister," I said. I was vaguely aware I sounded like a middle-aged mom from a television sit-com, but I couldn't help it. "Who was that guy?"

He shrugged. Oh hell no. I wanted more info than that. Actually, I was kind of desperate for it. Because for all the run-ins I'd ever had with men, I'd never met one that made me feel whatever was coursing through my bloodstream right then. Sure, I was angry, but also . . . excited.

He was hot. Hot and sexual and probably fucked a lot, given the way women flocked to those bad-boy types. He clearly thought a lot of himself.

And now here I was, thinking a lot of him, as well.

"What the fuck does that mean?" I probed deeper. "Who is he? He's in a different club than you are? Why are you with him? What is he—"

"Fuck!" he yelled, finally meeting my eyes. "Geez, Char. Give it a rest. He's just some guy from a different club who dropped me off. That's it."

I lowered my voice. The last thing I needed was him running out on me again. "And your phone died?"

"Yeah." He rolled his eyes. "We went over all this before. What else do you want from me?"

I sighed and sat down on the couch next to him. I reached out to him but he flinched away. "I want you to be honest with me. I'm not the enemy, here. I want you to be safe."

He stared into his cereal bowl. "I can take care of myself."

That was a load of bull. Yes, maybe he thought he could, and maybe I should be letting him make those mistakes, but with the people he was running with?

One mistake wouldn't just get him in trouble. It would get him killed. "I would think so, if you hadn't gotten involved with those guys. What's the allure, Jojo?"

He sighed. "For the last time, don't call me that!"

"Sorry," I said. He'd always been fine with the nickname, up until a few months ago. That was when all of this started. When he changed from my sweet brother to a total asshole. "Joel."

The word felt foreign on my lips. I'd never called him that. He didn't speak to answer my question, so I ventured more. "I mean, what about your medication? Did you take it?"

He shook his head. "It's bullshit."

"It's not bullshit, Joj—Joel. It's keeping you alive. You have asthma. You need to take it every day. I bet you don't even have your inhaler with you."

He stared at the ground. That was the answer to that. Well, great. Those tough men in leather jackets had such an allure to him that he was willing to die to hang out with them. I doubted they'd even care if he had an asthma attack and collapsed at their feet. They'd probably walk away and let him die. When did my smart brother abandon all sanity for this craziness?

I couldn't get it through my head. But talking to him was like pulling teeth, like I was just having a conversation with myself. I wanted desperately to understand, so I tried again.

"Is it because you're looking for friends? You did have friends before, remember? Chris, and Vin, and—"

"They went to college."

I blinked. I hadn't known that. "But you had a lot of friends. Surely, not all of them—"

"They're all fuckin' pussies." He snorted. "You don't get it, Char. You never will. These men are more like me. More like what I want to be."

I stared at him in horror. After everything I'd done to keep him out of trouble and raise him up with a good head on his shoulders? "No, I guess I don't get it. You want to be a biker?"

"It's not that."

"Well, where'd the gun come from, then?"

"One of the guys let me have it. I didn't . . . it was just to—"

"To run around with a gun shooting people and getting arrested? What? Do they sell drugs? Is that what you want? Have a rap sheet so that you'll never have a chance at a decent job again? Because I'll tell you, even Jack in the Box won't hire someone with a criminal record. You're throwing your life away for a bunch of hoodlums who like to parade around town, thinking they're tough shit, terrorizing innocent people. What kind of life is that?"

"That's not it. That's not what they do," he muttered.

I threw up my hands, exasperated. "Well, what do they do? Tell me so I can understand."

He shook his head and let out one of those surly laughs, just like the man at the curb. I hated that he was rubbing off on my little brother like that. "Forget it."

"No, I'm not just going to –"

"—Holy shit, Char!" he exploded suddenly, dropping his bowl and standing up. "I'm old enough to do stuff on my own and decide who I want to roll with. You don't have any say in it so just butt the fuck out!"

Then he stalked to his room and slammed the door.

I stared at Bert, my little mutt, who'd put his white paws up on my thigh. I stroked his little head, thinking. My body was trembling. As I sat there, I heard Jojo bitching to himself about how I'd gone through his room. God forbid I'd actually try to give him clean clothes.

I mean, hell. All I was trying to do was help him. Why was I suddenly the enemy? Anger pulsing through my veins, I got up and went to my bedroom, then threw myself down on my bed. I hadn't slept at all last night.

I rolled over and looked at the ceiling, thinking of that man in the parking lot. He was HOT, in all capital letters, no doubt about it. I cursed myself for dwelling on him, even if I knew why. I hadn't had sex in years. Not since that gang-bang when I worked at the store.

And though I'd gotten plenty of guys off, it hadn't exactly been all that fulfilling for me. Except for the money.

But that man—with his intense eyes and his muscular body and his blatantly sexual way of moving-- had awakened something in me. Lust. Need.

And I was horny.

Horny beyond all belief.

I sat up and decided I needed to take a shower. Right away. I needed to get myself off and then cool myself down.

Because the guy I wanted Jojo to stay as far away from as possible?

I wanted him all over me.

Chapter Nine

Hart

I headed back to my apartment to get some sleep, still thinking about that girl. Charlotte. She was so angry. Her brother was right—she was wound tight as a drum, probably didn't know a thing about fun. I smiled, wondering what she looked like when she smiled. Wondering when she'd smiled last.

I stopped at the Circle K to get some gas, and my phone buzzed. I lifted it to my ear. "Yeah?" Zain on the other end.

"Hey, Hart." His voice sounded strained and far away. That wasn't good. Zain was about the most calm and relaxed dude I knew.

I covered my other ear so the traffic from the highway wouldn't interfere and hunched over. "What's up?"

"I'm in the alley behind the old ribbon factory, off of Sunset. You know where that is?"

"Yeah. What's going on?"

"I was boosting that S-Class. You know, the white one we'd talked about?"

I did. I'd given Jet the tracker to put on it so Zain could make the pick-up, but I thought Cullen was going to have us wait on that one. He'd boosted it in broad daylight? That took some balls. "What's happening?"

"Two guys from the Fury spotted me, and I had to back up. I'm in the alley now, waiting for the coast to clear, but the guys ain't budging. I'm fucked. No way out."

Shit. I thought of what Joel had said about the Fury, keeping a close tail on us. If they had been doing that for some time, this was the first time they'd actually gotten in our way. It made me wonder just what they knew regarding Slade.

"I'll be there in five."

I finished pumping my gas and hopped on my bike, speeding to the old factory. When I got close, I cut the engine and coasted toward the intersection, where I edged in between two cars and saw the two guys from the Fury, parked in front of an alley.

Backing up, I rolled until I was a safe distance away and went around the block, entering the alley from the back way. I saw the problem immediately. The back of the alley was only wide enough to fit my bike. My shoulders nearly scraped the brick building. I rolled through to where the alley widened and saw Zain, sitting in the car, just as cool as could be, smoking a cigarette.

I squinted to the end of the alley. In the sunlight, I could see a couple of shapes, but nothing definitive. They were a long way off.

"Fancy meeting you here," I said to him, giving him a fist bump through the open window.

"Yeah. They're out there, right?"

I nodded. "What happened?"

He scrubbed a hand over his face. "I boosted the car. Business as usual. Then these two assholes ended up on my tail. I thought I could lose them by going down this alley. Didn't know it was a dead end. Tried to back out and they started shooting at me. So I shot back."

I scrubbed my jaw, assessing the situation. He couldn't back out. If he did, they'd start shooting, and probably destroy the car, possibly killing him. Couldn't go forward. The alley was too narrow.

Yeah, this was a problem.

"So. What the fuck do we do?"

My first thought: Leave the car. We were already fucked. There was no way out without going through those fuckers, and any time we spent with this car was time for the police to be alerted that the ride was missing and put a bulletin out for it. "We've got to go. Without the ride."

Zain nodded in agreement. "Fuck!" he muttered, banging his hand on the steering wheel. "Cullen ain't gonna like this."

"He'll understand."

Zain got out of the car and walked to the back of the car, where I'd parked my bike. He looked back at the S-Class and shook his head. "Damn shame. Nice car. Our client was looking out for that exact model."

I shrugged at him, "What can you do?" Our lives were more important. Plus, Aveline Bay was a wealthy coastal town and had no shortage of douchebags driving S-Classes. We'd get another chance. I led the bike out to the L-intersection, where I was able to turn it around.

The second he started to climb on the back of it, a bullet whizzed through the air, burying itself in the brick wall behind me. Dust from the smashed wall billowed into the air like smoke. "Shit! Get down!"

We both slid down to the ground, behind my bike and the car, and pulled out our guns. The bullet had come from the narrow alley, which meant one of them had gone around the block, where I'd come in.

We were trapped.

"Shit! What do they think they're doing?" Zain said, peering around the corner and leveling his gun just as another bullet tore past us, nearly giving him a close shave. "Holy fuck."

I fell to my belly and held the gun in front of me as I looked down the alley, underneath the chassis of the car. Just as I did, the window of the car exploded, raining glass onto me.

Great. Now they were shooting at us from both sides.

Zain sank down next to me, got off a shot, and started to reload. "We're fucked. They've got us surrounded."

Surrounded, and as I peered down the alley, seeing the shape of a man on a bike gradually getting clearer, I knew they were coming closer. Using the

Mercedes as my shield, I squeezed off a shot, but it didn't stop the guy from advancing.

Suddenly, I heard another sound, and not the adrenaline pulsing through my veins. It was far away, but unmistakable. Police sirens.

The other men heard it too, because they started to push off and retreat. Zain closed his eyes and breathed a sigh of relief, just as one of the men called, "We been watching you! You hear us? We know about Slade! You pussies better get ready 'cause we're coming for you!"

I eyed my bike. It hadn't been hit by any stray bullets. Then I motioned to Zain slightly with my chin. He got the idea. The second the Fury's motors started to scream away into the distance, we both dove for the bike. I gunned it and sailed out of the alley as fast as I could, making it out of there free and clear.

Zain pumped his fist. "Holy shit."

We drove for about a mile, until we knew we hadn't been followed. Then I pulled off to the side of the highway, and we both got off the bike, bending over with our hands on our knees, breathing hard. We needed a minute to calm the fuck down.

"They know," Zain finally said after a minute. "About Slade?"

I nodded. "Don't know."

"You think that kid told them?"

I shook my head. Yeah, the most logical answer was that Joel had seen the thing and somehow found time to report to the Fury, even though he'd said to me he hadn't. He could've been lying, but I didn't think so. The kid wasn't smooth enough for that.

"The kid did say they've been tracking us pretty close for a while. Maybe they saw something. Could've been any number of things."

Zain kicked at the dirt with his boot. "Shit."

"Hold on." I opened my phone so I could track what Joel had been doing for the past three hours since I left him. Nothing much. He'd ordered a sandwich from the Subway but didn't make any calls or send any texts. Other than that, he'd Googled one thing.

The Steel Cobras.

Well, that was interesting. He hadn't brought up much. We were pretty under the radar, as were most clubs. We didn't go around flying our flag for all to see.

But it was a good sign he was curious about us. It meant we were getting under his skin.

I lifted my phone up. "We need to get Cullen to call church. I've been talking with the kid. I think the brothers need to know that the Fury have been following us hardcore for a while."

"Yeah."

I got on the phone with Cullen, who answered with, "Yeah? What's going on with the kid?"

"The kid's back home, but I'm tracking his phone. Listen. We have bigger fish to fry right now."

"Yeah?"

"I just picked Zain up from the boost he was making. It went bad. We had to leave the car."

"You what?" I could hear the anger in his voice. "Shit. What happened?"

"The Fury happened. They boxed him in so we had to get away. When they were leaving, they called out to us that they knew about Slade and that we should prepare for a war."

"Fuck," Cullen breathed. "And you just let that kid go?"

"Listen to me. I don't think it was him," I said. "He told me they've been watching us hard for a few weeks. I don't think the kid's our man. I got him talking last night. He was pretty open about what he knew, after a while. Gave me a lot of intel."

"Yeah? All right. I want your asses back in the clubhouse in fifteen for church. I'll text the others."

He hung up, and I looked at Zain. "Church in fifteen."

We got back on my bike and headed to the pier. We were the first to arrive at the clubhouse, a rare thing for Zain, who'd never been on time for anything in his life. We went inside and tossed back a few beers as we waited for the rest of the guys to arrive.

The first thing out of Jet's mouth? "So what happened to the white S-class I tagged?"

Zain growled, "We had a problem. Fury."

Jet raised an eyebrow as he grabbed a chair and sat down. "Seriously? Those fuckers got in the way of making a pick? What the fuck?"

Cullen said, "Calm down, Jet. If I'm not mistaken, you're the one who fucked up on the last one. Remember the Ferrari?"

We all shifted our eyes from our beers, cigarettes, and grease-stained fingernails to Jet. We sure as hell all remembered the Ferrari. He was our tagger for the job but fucked up. He hadn't stuck my tracking device on the car firmly enough, and it fell off. Who knows how much money he torched on that dumbass move?

Miraculously, Jet shut up for once in his life. He looked down at his knuckles and leaned back in his chair.

"Yeah. We're not actually having a really good month when it comes to the business," Cullen said to us, scanning around the room. "Our overseas clients don't want to hear excuses."

"So what happened with the S-Class?" Nix asked.

Zain gave them all the rundown. When he finished, they all looked at him for a minute, not saying anything. Then Nix ran both hands down his face and shook his head. "Shit," he breathed. "So all we did to avoid them finding out about Slade was for nothing."

"Yep. Pretty much."

"So, what? Was it that kid?" Drake asked, dropping his beer bottle on the table.

"Nah, that's the thing," I said. "They've been tracking us hot and heavy for a while. I got the feeling the kid really didn't know anything about what Nix and

Jet were doing out there. He just saw the colors and started firing. Someone else must've seen something."

Jet took a drag of his cigarette. "You been keeping an eye on that kid?"

I smirked at him. "Yeah. No thanks to you."

He ignored the dig. "So what has he said? Anything?"

"Yeah. A lot, actually. He still seems pretty tight with wanting to be a Fury. But he did tell me a few things. Like that there's a new Veep, named Scar, who's been ordering them all to keep a watch on us. According to the kid, we're their number one target. This dude's pretty hot on watching us and finding a way to take us out. So Joel's been giving them intel on us for the past week."

Jet shook his head. "Of course they are. They've got nothing better to do. The kid tell you why he wants to be a part of that shit show?"

I shrugged 'cause I wasn't sure myself. "Looks like he's just looking for a place to fit in. He's kind of naïve.

Wants a family, and a friend suggested it to him. I get the feeling he went for it because it was all he knew. He doesn't seem to be married to the thought, though."

"Where is he now?" Nix asked.

"I let him go back home. Put a tracker on his phone so I could see where he was and record his conversations," I explained. "Hasn't done much on his phone though."

Jet squinted at me. "You just let him go? What the fuck for?"

I held up a hand to him. "Hey. In case you didn't notice. I'm not the fucking babysitter. If you wanted to keep him under lock and key twenty-four-seven, you could've volunteered to watch him last night instead of going on your booty call."

He crossed his arms. "Maybe I should have. I sure as hell wouldn't have just let him go!"

"You're the one who wanted to turn him to our side. Keeping him on a leash ain't the way to do that, Jet. You know that," I muttered.

Jet glared at me but said nothing. Good. Because he was about five seconds away from getting my fist in his face.

"All right, guys, break it up," Cullen muttered, looking at me. "This isn't good. How do we know we can trust that this kid is giving us the straight shit? Maybe he's giving us bad intel."

"He could be, but I doubt it." I held up my phone. "Look. I'm monitoring him through his phone. If he does anything out of line, we know where to find him. I made it clear we weren't going to let him go. I think he got the picture. He's scared."

"Yeah. But we gotta know for sure," Nix put in.

Cullen hitched his chin at me. "Can you get on the kid? See if you can shore up what side he's on and if he's just playing with us?"

I could feel my eyebrows narrowing, trying to figure out how the fuck to do that. But whatever, once again, Hart to the rescue, taking care of the little newb. I guess if Jet took over this job the kid would've already gone running back to the Fury camp, and we'd be looking at all-out war by now.

So I'd do it. Besides, it'd give me a chance to see that spitfire of a sister again. "I'll try," I said. Ignoring Jet.

When Cullen adjourned the meeting, I went out to my bike, checking my phone to see what Joel had been up to. Not much. He'd posted a close-up picture of his bicep, baring another kind of pathetic tattoo with the caption: Good workout today.

Well, that was good. Our little boy was behaving himself.

I quickly rang his number. He answered on the first ring. "Hey."

"Joel? It's Hart."

"Oh. Hey."

I could sense him stiffening. Good. He needed to have respect for us. It was better than his earlier tough guy act, where he'd called us some pretty fucked up names.

"What's up?"

"I told you to be ready 'cause I was gonna need you," I said, grabbing my helmet. "Well . . . I need to talk to you."

"Okay. Sure. I'm at my house." Yes, he was. I knew that already. "You want to come by here? My sister's been on a rampage, yelling at me every two seconds. I need to get the fuck out of here."

"Yeah. That sounds good. Be there in five," I said, hanging up.

I wasn't looking forward to dragging shit out of the Fury prospect, but for some reason, I couldn't wait to see that feisty girl.

EVIE MONROE

Chapter Ten

Charlotte

On my way to the shower, I could hear Joel pumping iron. That was fine. Healthy. I was glad he was doing that and not anything that could get him in trouble.

But he had to clean his room. And . . . we still needed to talk about the gun. I wanted him to surrender it to whoever he'd gotten it from. While I showered, I decided that the best way to do that would be to offer him some kind of incentive. Like, if he got a real job and got rid of the gun, I'd let him stay at my place rent-free, no questions asked. If he kept things in order, I wouldn't go snooping through his room. That kind of thing.

Listening through the door to his heavy breathing and the weights clinking together, I grabbed a post-it and wrote, LET'S TALK!, then stuck it on the door. We were both so busy with different schedules these days, that was how we communicated.

Then I went back to my bedroom to get ready for work. I had the late shift, which meant I'd be at the vets until midnight, so I got into my pink scrubs, threw my hair into a ponytail, and went down to the kitchen to get some dinner.

As I walked down the hall, I heard the shower running. Then I realized my post-it note wasn't on his door. My eyes scanned to the threadbare carpet and saw it crumpled on the ground.

So, that pretty much answered that question. He was still pissed at me.

Fine, I thought. I'd just go to work. Before I left, though, I'd make him promise to stay home. He had to. He couldn't keep going out, night after night. Wasn't he exhausted?

When the water shut off, I waited for him in the hall eating a Hot Pocket. He appeared in the doorway, towel around his waist, his hair hanging down over his eyes and water droplets on his bony shoulders. I pounced.

"You're staying home tonight!" I ordered.

"Jesus!" He took a step back. Then he rolled his eyes and pushed past me, toward his room. At least he smelled good.

"I'm serious!" I shouted after him.

His answer? He slammed the door in my face. I let out a groan as I clenched my hands into fists. So this was how he was going to play it. My little brother, who never used to hold a grudge longer than ten minutes, was now giving me the silent treatment. Damn him. That was my tactic.

I went back to the kitchen, finished up my Hot Pocket and lemonade by myself. Then I went to the bathroom and brushed my teeth. As I was gargling, I heard the sound of a motorcycle coming closer.

Oh. Hell. No. Not happening. No way was I—

Before I could make a move, Jojo's door opened. Now fully dressed in baggy jeans and a t-shirt, he strode purposefully, with his head down, to the door, like he was trying to avoid someone.

Me, of course.

"Hold it!" I shouted at him, the words garbled because I hadn't yet spit.

He didn't stop. He ignored me, throwing open the door and letting it slam behind him.

Who the fuck did he think he was?

I rinsed my toothpaste out, threw my toothbrush in the sink, then raced out after him. I tore open the door and dashed down the stairs, just in time to see Joel glance at me, then tear off into the night.

The guy he was with? The same hot, dirty guy as before. The one that made my insides do all kinds of crazy dances. I ran into the street, holding my hands out to block the guy from going any farther.

Really, it was a pathetic attempt at a blockade. The street was so wide he could've easily swerved either way around me. But he didn't. He stopped, his motorcycle roaring underneath him.

"What do you think you're doing? Where are you taking him?"

He tapped his ear and shrugged, then cut the engine on his bike. "Couldn't hear you, baby. What?"

I fisted my hands on my hips. "Don't act all innocent! You know very well I told you not to come around here and to leave Jojo alone!"

He rose to his feet and lifted his leg up, then stepped off his bike toward me. "I know you said that. But I think *Jojo* told you that he's old enough to make his own decisions."

I shook my head adamantly. "What the fuck do you know? You didn't raise him on your own since he was twelve, did you?"

He didn't answer. That amused smile threatened to come back, with those killer dimples. I steeled myself against it and added, "Did you?"

He held out his hands in surrender. "No, I did not, Charlotte."

My entire body tingled at the way he said my name. So sensually and sexually, it made me wish he'd say it again. Which was definitely not how I needed to react right now. And how did he know my name? Was Joel talking about what a no-fun stick-up-the-ass I was?

"Well," I said, lifting my chin. "Then you'll kindly butt out of our family business."

He laughed. "I would. But in case you haven't noticed, your brother is already gone."

I whirled around. He did have a point. The parking lot was empty. I'd thought that if he was going to go anywhere, he'd need this man to lead him. "Where did he go?"

"I know," he said, like it was a big secret he was holding over me.

"And . . .? Are you going to tell me?"

He tapped the side of his head, pretending to think.

I scowled at him. "You want your balls kneed again?"

"Fine," he sighed. "I asked him to come to our clubhouse. I need to discuss some business with him."

"Business? What kind of business?" He just shook his head. Oh, so it was top secret, motorcycle-man business. How stupid. Like I cared. I checked my phone. "Well. Will he be back by his curfew? Ten o'clock. I have to go to work?"

Then he really did start to laugh. "Your brother has a curfew?"

I nodded. "What's wrong with that?"

"He's nineteen, Charlie. An adult."

I opened my mouth to tell him that I didn't care if he was fifty, he was still my responsibility, when it hit me, just what he'd called me. "Did you just call me . . . *Charlie*?"

"Yeah. You got a problem with it?"

"Yes! Don't call me that . . . what is your name? Hart? What is that short for? Heartless?"

"It's my road name," he said. "Better than my real name. I like Charlie. You definitely look like a Charlie."

I snorted. "Well, you look like a stupid motherfucker. Can you please tell me where I can go to find my brother?" I said reached into the pockets of my pants for my keys. "Because I need to be at work in an hour—"

"Don't tell me you're going to go down there and bring him home?"

I nodded. "Why?"

"You think he'll ever forgive you if you do that?"

I froze, my hands on my hips. I was so annoyed, I was only half-listening. "Do what?"

"Show up to our club like his mommy and drag him home," he said with a laugh.

I sighed. He did have a point. I was already on thin ice with my little brother. I didn't want him to hate me any more than he already did. He might never come home and then I'd really be alone. "What do you suggest?"

He thought for a minute. "How about this? You let him live his life. And I'll get his ass home by . . . not ten. He's not a little kid. Say, midnight?"

I stared at him. "You will? Seriously?"

He held up his hand in an oath, then held it out for me. "I promise. It's a deal."

I reached over to shake it, but then I remembered something. "I have to take him his pill. He has asthma. If he doesn't take it every day, he could have a bad attack."

He nodded. "All right. Give it to me. I'll make sure he takes it."

"You will?" This seemed like a lot to entrust to a guy I barely knew who clearly was not health or safety minded, considering the death trap he'd chosen as his form of transportation. Still, I didn't have much of a choice. "You understand it's a life or death thing? It's not optional."

"Yeah. Got it." He didn't sound dismissive. That was refreshing.

I pointed to my apartment. "It's just inside." I started to run into the apartment with him right behind me. "And you are sure you'll get him to come home, at midnight?"

"Yeah."

I shoved open the door to the apartment and rushed in, the animals jumping at my feet in excitement. As I jogged to the bathroom, I called, "Close the door so the animals won't get out, please."

I reached into the medicine cabinet and found the bottle, peeled off the lid and shook a single tablet into my palm. I heard the door click closed.

Good. Maybe he wasn't such a bad guy, after all.

I set the bottle down on the shelf and grabbed one of Jojo's inhalers right beside it. He hadn't had to use it in ages, but that was when he was taking his pills regularly. Better to be safe than sorry.

I whirled around to head back into the living room and ran straight into bulging pectorals, a complete wall of a man. I breathed in sharply. He smelled of soap. And leather. And man, all man.

I hadn't expected him to come this far into my home. My eyes trailed up to meet his. All the air left the room, making it impossible to breathe. I lifted the pill.

"Got it," I said. "I'll wrap it in a tissue for you."

Anything to avoid those eyes of his.

I plucked a tissue out of the box on the counter and set about my work, trying to ignore his presence. He was so close; I could turn my head and be near enough to kiss him. I unfolded the tissue and carefully wrapped up the pill, my fingers trembling the whole time.

He had to notice. Him? He was as cool as ever, his breathing slow, deep, and methodical, his posture relaxed and devil-may-care as he slumped against the doorjamb.

I held the nicely wrapped package up to him in my palm.

He just stared at it. No . . . he wasn't staring at the pill. He was staring at me, into my eyes, with an intensity that made my knees weak. Eyes holding mine, he slowly reached out, took the pill and tucked it into the pocket of his jeans.

This was my apartment. And he'd instantly made me feel like I was the guest here. I gnawed on my lip and held up the inhaler. "Can you give this to him, too? Just in case?"

He took it in his hand, then backed against the wall and looked down. "Fuck."

I followed his line of sight. Mags, my giant white bunny, was running circles around his boots on the embarrassingly dirty shag carpet.

Oh, my gosh. Big man scared of a little rabbit. I crouched down to pick her up, then put my nose to hers to say hello.

"It's nothing, it's just Mags," I said, holding her up for an introduction. "Want to say hello?"

The corner of his mouth rose in disgust. "No."

I stroked her soft fur. Sometimes, petting my bunny was all I needed to relax me. But suddenly, Hart looked about as uptight as I'd ever seen him. "She must like you. She doesn't usually give greetings to people."

He looked down the hall, where Opie eyed him suspiciously from the top of the sofa. "What the fuck, are you running a zoo around here?"

"You don't like animals?" I asked as I kissed the top of Mag's head, crouched, and set her free.

He scratched his jaw and pocketed the inhaler in his jacket.

"Not at all."

Talk about a deal-breaker. I always said to myself that if I ever wanted to settle down, the guy would have to love animals. This guy was wrong for me in so many ways.

Not that I imagined a man like Hart ever wanting to settle down.

"Really? What do you have against them?"

He hitched a shoulder like he hadn't thought about it, took a step toward the door, and Mags followed him, doing her rounds so close to his boots that she nearly tripped him. He stopped. "Fucking insane rat. You like tripping over them like this?"

I bristled. "I don't trip." And to myself. *She's not a rat.*

He chuckled a little to himself, then turned to leave. "Whatever. I'll have Joel back at midnight."

I crossed my arms. "Good. See that you do. I swear, I'll come after you if you don't."

He rolled his eyes, unimpressed by the threat, and crossed the living room, scanning the ground to keep from tripping over the animals, curious by his presence.

"Oh! Make sure he takes it with food!" I called after him. He kept going, opening the door and stepping outside, so I found myself rushing to catch up to him. This was important info; if Jojo took it on an empty stomach, it was liable to make him sick. As I lunged forward, Mags got in my way, and I ended up sidestepping to avoid her, which made me knock my shin into the coffee table.

"Ouch!" I yelped and went flying.

Before I could even think, or put my hands out to break my fall, Hart wheeled back inside, caught me in his arms and lifted me against his chest. Out of breath, I murmured, "Thanks."

"You don't trip, huh?"

"Well, I—"

Now he was way too close for comfort. Touching me. Holding me. And he didn't appear to want to let go. He plucked and lifted a little of the fabric of my pink scrubs shirt off my collarbone. "You going to work? What do you do?" I was panting like a dog in heat. Dogs. Right. "Um, oh. I'm a vet tech."

A smile rose between his cinnamon whiskers, the hint of pure white teeth. He was delicious. I inhaled deeply again and nearly licked my lips.

Then I realized I was in his arms, and he was staring at my lips now, like they were his last meal. I struggled to find my footing and get out of his way. He set me upright, on my own feet, and I went to fluff my hair and explain that usually I didn't, but when I turned to look at him, the intention in his eyes was too much to resist.

He slammed his mouth on mine. *Fuck. Fuck. Fuck. He even tastes delicious.*

The force of it pushed me backward, and I was stumbling all over the apartment, but I didn't care. He pushed me up against the nearest wall and dove into my mouth, his tongue hard and insistent.

And that was when it hit me. This monster of a man was kissing me.

Not kissing. Devouring. As much as I wanted to say no and push him away, a part of me couldn't get enough. I didn't know if we could have stopped. If a freight train could've torn us apart. He went all in, open-mouthed, so I opened my mouth too and let him feed me his tongue, fuck me with his tongue.

My world upended. I'd never been kissed like this before. He ground his powerful body into me as he caged me against the now-closed front door, totally owning me.

He broke the kiss with a tortured breath and gazed at me with heavy-lidded, hungry eyes. "You want me," he breathed into my neck.

It was more of a statement than a question, and he knew the answer. All I could do was nod like a bobble-head. But he wasn't waiting for my permission. He kissed me deeper, harder, his hands roving up my sides to my breasts. I slid my tongue into his mouth to taste him, and before I could get my fill, he reached down and lifted me up, upending my world and making me dizzy.

I gasped into his mouth as I felt him walking me down the hall. Like he owned the place.

I didn't have any doubt. He was taking me to bed.

He didn't need directions. He got me inside my bedroom and closed the door with his foot. I heard Ernie whine outside as I never went to bed without including them, my favorite pillows. But for the first time, I didn't care. I'd been living in this apartment for years and not once had I ever fucked on my bed.

Fuck it. I was going to do it, now. In my apartment. Like a real, fucking adult.

He dropped me on my neatly made, flowered comforter. A second later, he reached for the tie of my pants, and undid it with one easy pull. Then, lifting my legs, he pulled my loose pants to my ankles, lifted them off, and tossed them over his shoulder. I sat up on my elbows, reaching for his jeans. I opened the snap and unzipped his pants, then I slipped my hand in there and pulled his dick out

Before I could wrap my fingers around it completely, he slid a hand under the small of my back and flipped me around, like a dog, so that I was on my hands and knees, my face in the comforter. He leaned over me, and I felt the length of his cock brush the crack of my ass, slowly, making my body flare with tingles. He felt so good. "You want this? You want me inside you?"

A nod again, one I wasn't sure my brain had control of. My body was calling the shots now.

The next thing I knew, I heard the rip of a condom package. So prepared. I was too far gone to be thinking rationally, so I was glad he was, even though every pore was screaming, *Give it to me*! *Now*! Fuck the consequences.

And then he did. He pushed inside me, so hard I let out all the air in my lungs in one gasp. He didn't stay in for long. He fucked me hard, grabbing my ponytail.

He leaned over and bit my ear. "This what you wanted?" his voice was a hard rasp.

The nod again.

"Yeah? Say something."

"Ye-es!" I said, my voice broken by the way he was riding me, so hard and rhythmic, I felt equal amounts pain and pleasure. His hot skin against mine, his enormous cock. I wasn't one to ever get pleasure from sex with another man. Honestly didn't know that I could, which was probably why I hadn't had it in years.

But this man? He'd broken that barrier. Now, I was heading full-steam ahead to my very first from-intercourse orgasm.

My toes and fingers went numb as all sensation began to center on the place where he met me, again and again and again. He gripped me around my belly and dragged me closer, still pulling my ponytail taut, but I pressed my face against my comforter and let out a strangled scream as it reached a fever pitch and I went off.

When I did, he changed rhythm, gripping me to him, then slowly feeding me his cock, inch by inch, like he was savoring the way my body contracted around his. Then he picked up rhythm again, growled, lifted me up, and set me down on my back as he came. He pumped again, retriggering my orgasm and making me feel like I'd lost every bone in my body.

When he finished, I was aware he was looking at me, his face in my face, all I could see . . . and yet I couldn't meet his eyes. I looked at his chin, and at the space between us, as he pulled out and sat on the mattress.

I sat up and reached for my pants. "I . . . don't know what just happened."

He chuckled in that same, easy way. "I think it's called fucking."

Uh, duh. Actually, the whole thing was a great big *duh*. What the fuck was I thinking only five minutes ago? I was insane. "Yes, but I don't do that."

"You saying you didn't enjoy yourself?" He looked back at me, but I averted his eyes again. "I know you did."

He was right, I definitely did. It wasn't insane. It was . . . good. He'd given me exactly what I needed, right when I needed it. And I wanted it. I couldn't resist it. But how some man I barely met, a man I actually hated, could do that to me . . . well, it just went to show that my sex life was ridiculously fucked up.

"It's . . . fine." I didn't want to give him too much credit. Everything about him—from that sexy smirk to that attitude-strut of his, told me he knew he had magical fucking powers. "I'm just trying to explain to you that I don't know what came over me. I'm not one to have sex with people I just met." *Not unless they're paying.*

He peeled the condom off his dick and, twisting it closed, zipped up his pants and pulled the front hem of his shirt down, like he was ready to leave.

"That's all right," he called after me.

Was he fucking kidding me? I grabbed my pants and jumped into them, both feet at once, then rushed to follow him. I found him in the kitchen, looking around for the trash. "I wasn't apologizing," I snapped.

He held up the used condom by the top. "Little help?"

I pointed under the sink. Then I realized that even though Jojo wasn't fond of throwing things away, if he found that condom, or—where the fuck was the wrapper?—he'd throttle me. He'd brought this guy home, I'd told him to stay away from him, and . . . then I went and rubbed myself all over him like a horny fucking nymph.

"Just . . ." I rushed to him and took the condom, then opened the trash and stuffed it way down in the bottom, under the morning's coffee grounds. "Do not tell Jojo."

"Wouldn't think of telling *Jojo*," he said with a smirk. "Hell. You really got some leash on him."

I frowned. "Obviously not a short enough one, considering he's been hanging out with the likes of you."

"And I'm so bad? I just had my cock inside you, baby. Made you cream all over me. There's got to be something about the likes of me that you like."

I shoved the trashcan closed and looked up at him. He was giving me that same, smug smirk, those light eyes boring into me, nailing me against the wall. "Nope."

He raised an eyebrow.

I crossed my arms. "I was really hard up. That's all. So thanks for the O. But that's all I needed."

He gave me a suspicious look. "Oh, yeah? No boyfriend? No hot veterinarians where you work?"

I shook my head. "I don't have time for a man."

"You just did. It didn't take that long, did it?"

Yeah. It'd taken about fifteen minutes from the time I'd come up to the bathroom to the time he was pulling out of me. I'm not sure I could've even accomplished that with my very best vibrator. I felt my face blushing as I was drawn back there, and suddenly it hit me. I had to be at work. I looked at the clock on the oven. "Shit. I've got to get to work."

I started to rush past him, but he spread one thick, muscle-bound arm across the doorway, effectively barring my way. I pushed on it, but it didn't budge.

"What are you . . . I've got to go."

"You ever been late?"

"No, and I don't plan to," I said, as he put a finger under my chin and tilted my face up to his.

"You know what's better than a good O, baby?"

I shook my head, my pulse racing in anticipation at finding out.

"Two of them. And I think you can be a little late, baby," he said.

This time, when he swept in to capture my lips, he brushed his across them gently, licking, playing, teasing.

And I knew I was never going to make it into work on time.

Chapter Eleven

Hart

I didn't have another condom.

That was all right.

There was something so sexy about Charlotte when she finally let go and came. Her face got all tense and then this sweet look of pure relaxation passed over her, finally, for the briefest of times, freeing her from that prison of a life she was in. So if this was my last chance to claim Jojo's high-strung sister before she finally came to her senses, I wasn't going to waste it.

I carried her back to her bedroom, closing the animals out, and stripped her completely naked.

This time, I stood back to appreciate her. She was fucking phenomenal. Easily the best looking girl I'd ever seen. I spread her legs and stood between her naked body as she gazed at me in eager anticipation, gnawing on her lip.

Sure, she never did this kind of thing. But I could already sense she was one of those girls. The ones who professed to be good, until I got them home and they became total freaks in bed.

My favorite kind.

I dove in, spreading her lips apart and zeroing right on her clit with my tongue. She let out a gasp and tried to close her legs, but I held them firm.

"I don't . . ." she started, but I silenced her by sucking the little nub into my mouth, running my tongue over it.

She had no other protest after that. A second later, she had her feet on my shoulders and was lifting her ass up to meet my face, grinding herself into me.

She tasted sweet. I loved that this girl who hated me so much was so wet and ready for me. I loved the little whimpers she made. I could fucking do this all day.

The moment she started to come, I pushed my finger up into her hot, slick cunt, feeling her insides contract, again and again.

When she was done, she pushed up off of me. "All right, really, stop it," she said, out of breath, and with no resignation at all. "I've got to get to work."

I wiped her juices off my face with the back of my hand. "If you wanted me to stop, you could have told me before I made you come."

She gave me a guilty look. Nah, she'd wanted it too much; she couldn't deny it. She grabbed her pants, and pulled them on, glancing at the clock on the night table. "Ugh. I'm going to be so late."

Her room was all pink and flowers, like a little kid. I sat on the bed and watched her as she grabbed a sweater from the closet. "Want a ride?"

She whirled. "On your death trap? No thanks, I'll take my car."

Right. "Sorry. Thought maybe coming a few times would dislodge that stick from your ass."

She scowled at me. "Oh, is that what your plan was? Well, you're wrong. Go and get my brother. Watch him, like you promised. Don't let him out of your sight."

I saluted.

"Seriously. If anything bad happens to him, I'm coming after you. And it won't be pretty." She shrugged her sweater on, threw open the door of the bedroom, and when I didn't move, motioned with her chin. "Come on."

I pushed off the bed and followed her toward the door. She reached the doorknob and stopped. "And you won't forget to give him the pill?"

Whatever coming did for her, it definitely didn't calm her down any. "Yeah. I'll give him the pill the second I see him. Jesus, baby, are you always this uptight?"

She let out a long breath and fell against the wall for a moment. "Well. I have to be. He's making stupid decisions and I don't want to get a call from the hospital telling me to come identify his body."

I couldn't argue with that. Getting tangled with the Fury and shooting at Cobras wasn't the brightest thing he could've done. "I'll watch after him."

"Thanks. Are . . . are the men he went to see okay? They won't hurt him, will they?"

I shook my head. "They're my brothers. I texted them to let him into the clubhouse. They're waiting for me now."

I held up my phone so she could see the messages I'd gotten from Cullen, wondering where they hell I'd gone off to. I'd managed, while she was putting on her pants the first time, to tell him I'd be a little late.

She read the words and sucked in a breath. "You promise you won't tell Jojo about this?"

No fucking way. The trust I had with the kid was tentative enough. It wouldn't last if he knew what I'd just been doing with his sister. That would fuck up everything we'd been trying to do with the Hell's Fury. "Promise."

"And you'll take care of him? I know I'm crazy, and overbearing, and—what did you say, just a minute ago? Oh, uptight." She shrugged. "Guilty as charged. But he's really the only family I have. And he's a good kid. He's had it tough, and it's not his fault."

"I'll guard him like my own brother." That, I would do. Not just for her. Because if the Fury got their hands on him, I wasn't sure what would happen.

"Great." For about a split second, I thought I saw a smile on her face, but she whirled around so fast to face the living room, I couldn't be sure.

She looked at her animals and blew them all kisses. I could peg her for one of those types who dressed their pets in Halloween costumes and let them have their run of her bed. Fuck no. "I'll be back," she cooed to them sweetly, the exact opposite of the voice she used with me. "Be good!"

She let me out the door and closed it. As we walked to the parking spot, her head was down. And I knew exactly what she was thinking.

When we got to the curb, she spoke, and I was right. "Listen. Hart. What happened in there. Maybe I needed it. But . . . that doesn't mean it should keep happening. It can't. For Jojo's sake . . . and mine."

I dug my hands into the pockets of my jeans. Beyond the little tissue-wrapped pill Charlotte had given me, I found my keys. "Yours?"

She nodded. "Like I said. I have enough on my plate, just trying to keep my brother straight. I don't need men to complicate my life."

I couldn't say I hadn't expected that. It was why I'd gone in for that second taste. But, I knew eventually she'd change her mind.

But that didn't mean she wouldn't change her mind back again. "Okay, Charlie."

She scowled. Okay, so, giving her two sorely needed orgasms hadn't bought me any brownie points where that was concerned.

"Charlotte." I scoffed.

"Thank you. Your phone all charged?"

I lifted it. "Ninety percent."

"Good." She looked at a little piece of shit car that must have been hers, and then awkwardly reached out her hand to shake mine.

I stared at it. I felt like I'd just sold her a used car, and now we were agreeing to the deal. Had she forgotten I'd just had my tongue up her cunt? She was a funny little mystery.

It kind of fucking turned me on. So I decided to humor her. I shook it. Her hand was cold, her posture rigid.

I wondered how many times I'd have to make her come to get her to loosen that hot little body of hers up.

HART

Whatever that number was? Shit, I was ready. I'd had a taste of her and now, it would never be enough.

EVIE MONROE

Chapter Twelve

Charlotte

When I slid into the driver's seat of my car, I felt like banging my head against the steering wheel.

In fact, I almost did, until I realized that my hot, bad, totally-wrong-for-me biker dude was still straddling his bike, looking at me, waiting for me to pull out. What a gentleman.

So I did, cringing the whole time. When he sailed off toward the harbor, I realized my hands were shaking on the steering wheel.

I couldn't believe I fucked him. I'd never fucked a complete stranger like that. Even the guys in the produce department had all been at least known to me.

Not only that. I'd learned my lesson so well the first time, I let him go down on me and make me come a second time.

As I pressed on the accelerator, I wasn't sure that, even with all the doubt and regret swirling in my head, I'd be able to turn him down for a third.

Holy Mary Mother of God. I had to get control of my overheated ass before I had a car accident.

I drove toward the office, wondering how I was going to focus on my job. I wrapped my hands around the steering wheel so hard to keep them from shaking that my knuckles turned white. So I concentrated on my breathing.

Really, what was my problem? I'd dealt with men with massive egos all my life. Of course, none remotely as hot as Hart. I'd never let them get the best of me, especially where Jojo was concerned. He'd always been my top priority. If I saw anyone fucking with him, I gave them hell. So what had started out that way—as me trying to give that fucker hell--somehow wound up getting me lost along the way.

And I ended up with my legs wrapped around him. My pussy *creaming* all over him.

Talk about a wrong turn.

I glanced at myself in the rearview mirror and growled in disgust at my reflection. Ugh. I looked guilty. Like a spineless sap. I'd always been so proud of the way I handled myself where my little brother was concerned. Like, even if I had to make sacrifices or do something beneath me, at least it was for his own good.

But what was this?

This was me, thinking only of me for once. I never did that. But the way he felt inside me? Pounding me. Sliding all that delicious cock inside of me. God he felt good.

But I couldn't think about that right now, especially when Jojo needed me most. I needed to concentrate on him. This was a crucial time in his life, and I had to be there for him, even if he didn't think he wanted me there.

Really, if he was messed up in this motorcycle club stuff, probably the best thing we could do was move away. Especially now, since I was messed up with them, as well. Well, not *them*—just one of them, but it was enough. We could go north, to another town that didn't have bikers to worry about.

But I'd checked before, and the rent was almost twice what it was for my apartment. We were barely scraping by with my salary. How could we afford that? I'd have to get two jobs and then who would keep an eye on my brother?

Drumming my fingers on the steering wheel as I sat at a red light, I wondered what we could do. Right now, my savings were dismal—I could barely put away five bucks a week after paying for the necessities. At least I had a savings account, but it had less than a hundred bucks in it, and I'd been saving for months.

Maybe I could find a job that paid more. There was only one vet in Aveline Bay, but I'd heard of other places, especially rural areas where people had a lot of animals, that might offer more hours and pay better.

That was what I needed to do. Find something else, somewhere else.

I made a mental note to scour the jobs online, as soon as I got off work at midnight.

I pulled into the parking lot of the veterinarian, where only a couple of cars were parked. Tonight would be easy because I wouldn't have to deal with regular appointments. I'd just work with the animals staying in the kennels overnight, making sure that they were okay and the ones who'd recently had surgeries weren't having trouble.

It'd be easy and . . . boring.

Meaning, plenty of time for my mind to wander.

To Hart.

Which I really didn't want it to do. But it seemed like whatever I turned my mind to, images of Hart came back. They were always right there, threatening to bubble to the surface.

What was it that had gotten me so stuck on him? Was it that fuck-you, aloof, don't-care attitude? I thought I hated that bad-boy shit.

Apparently not, since Hart had it in spades.

I took the key out of the ignition and looked at my phone. I had one text, from Jojo. *At the clubhouse. Hart told me to text you. Back by midnight.*

I smiled. Good. Hart may have been a bad-boy, but he had kept his promise, and was making Jojo toe the line so he wouldn't make me insane. At least I had that.

But as I got out of the car, a feeling of dread washed over me. I usually loved my job, but now I wanted to be home.

In my bed.

With Hart on top of me.

My skin prickled with goosebumps as I thought of the way he'd pretty much owned my body.

Fuck me. Why was I such a pathetic loser? I was actually jealous of my little brother for getting to spend time with Hart, the same guy I'd been warning him to stay away from. What was wrong with me?

Head hanging, tail between my legs, I went into the office and breathed a sigh of relief when I saw Barb, the other tech working the late shift. She was a forty-something divorced mother of two. She and I actually had a lot in common because Jojo was about the same age as her youngest son. I liked Barb. She wasn't all about parties and manicures, like some of the younger techs. I said hello to the doctor on call in the back before putting my late-night snack in the break-room refrigerator and setting my purse in my locker.

Then I went to the little bunny cages to see how Flopsy was doing. The sweet little bunny wasn't there.

I looked around, tapping my chin,. Where was the poor bunny with the GI infection? I hoped he hadn't had any complications. I meandered out front, where we kept the small animals up for adoption.

I breathed a sigh of relief when I spotted him in a new cage. He looked up at me as I reaching in with my finger in to pet the soft spot between his ears.

I grinned from ear-to-ear when I saw the sticker that said I'M ADOPTED! on his cage. "Barb! Someone adopted him!" I said, clapping my hands.

Then I looked around and realized Barb had gone into the back.

We weren't busy so I played with the bunny, teasing him with my finger so he'd wiggle that cute little pink nose of his. I couldn't believe people like Hart, who didn't completely melt when they looked at cute little animals. What the fuck was wrong with him?

I groaned to myself. And why was I thinking about him *again*?

I tried to tuck him in the back of my mind while I turned around to the sound of Barb coming out of the back room.

"Are you feeling all right?" she asked me.

I felt my face, which hadn't really recovered since my little adventure with Hart. It still felt hot and feverish. "Yeah. Why? Do I look funny?"

That was when I saw the bright aqua case that looked suspiciously like my phone. Where the heck did she get that? I knew I'd taken it out of my purse because

I always carried it with me at work, so I wouldn't miss any texts from Jojo.

She asked with a smile, "Are you trying to get more cold calls?"

Confused, I looked down and realized my mistake. I thought I'd put my snacks in the fridge, but actually, I'd actually carried them out with me. And my phone?

Well, of course, I'd put it in the fridge.

Duh.

I grabbed my phone from her. "Sorry. I really probably shouldn't be trusted tonight," I said to her with an apologetic shake of the head.

"We've all been there," she called after me as I went to put my snacks where they belonged.

Sure, maybe we all had been there. But I was the only dumbass who was there because I'd been fucking around with a man that I needed to run away from, as fast and as far as I could.

EVIE MONROE

Chapter Thirteen

Hart

By the time I reached the clubhouse, the kid had been waiting a while. Which wasn't the best idea considering we were trying to keep our association with him out of the Fury's eyes. Luckily, some of the guys had shown up and let him in. Cullen, Drake, Zain and Jet were there, shooting pool.

The first thing I did was give him his pill. I made him wash it down with a full glass of water and a handful of crackers I'd found in one of the cabinets. Then I told him to text his warden and put her mind at ease. He'd been sitting in a chair away from the rest of the guys, trading suspicious glances with them, so he was glad to follow my directions.

When he finished and had successfully warned off his hot little keeper, I dragged his chair into the fray and took an empty one next to him. "All right. Talk to us. The Fury contact you today?"

He looked at his lap and gave us a nod.

Glad to see he was telling the truth. I knew they had, though he didn't know I knew. I'd called Cullen and reported to him earlier all the calls going to and from Joel's phone. He'd gotten one from someone whose name wasn't mentioned, but if he didn't tell us, I could probably look it up. They'd talked about the Fury finding Slade's body and how pissed they were. They'd asked him why he was MIA. During the conversation, he hadn't said anything to give them any impression that he was working with us.

"And?"

He shrugged. "They told me they'd found Slade's body and asked if I thought you guys had anything to do with it. I said I didn't know."

I chewed on my lip. Good. This all checked out.

"They asked me where the hell I'd been. I told them my sister was having issues and I was dealing with her. That's all."

Cullen looked over at me. I nodded at him to let him know the kid was telling the truth. Cullen asked, "You think they believe you?"

Joel nodded. "Sure. They don't have any reason not to."

"All right," I said. "Good job."

"Yeah," Cullen added. "Just keep it up. Keep deflecting whenever you can, and you'll come out of this all right, kid."

Across the table, Jet nodded smugly, like his idea of turning the kid to our side wasn't the result of all of my hard work. Asshole.

"So what now?" Zain asked.

Cullen shrugged. "We just keep doing our thing like we ain't done nothing wrong and never saw Slade." He looked at Drake. "Cait and Roxanne okay?"

Slade's family. Drake nodded. "Yeah. No one's come looking around my place for them. But they're worried that if they ever do show their faces around town, they'll get the Fury's wrath. Even if the Fury doesn't think we're responsible, they'll think they are."

Cullen took a drag of his cigarette and blew it out. "Which is why I don't want them leaving your place until this is over."

Drake frowned. "They're restless."

Cullen shrugged. "Better restless than dead. Which is what they'll be if they leave our protection. You tell them that."

He nodded.

"Just a couple more weeks," Cullen said coolly.

I doubted that. I didn't see Slade's wife and daughter being safe in this town ever again, as long as the Fury existed. He disappeared and so did they. It was easy to make the association. It wasn't like they'd simply let their president's murder just slide.

After that, we all stood. Before I could talk to Joel, Cullen called me over and asked me to talk to him in private for a little bit. We went to a corner of the warehouse and he said, "So really. How's it going?"

"Good. Like I said, he's been in touch with the Fury, but he's being honest about everything he's doing."

"You think the Fury suspects anything?"

I shook my head. "Not yet. I mean, they've been keeping an eye on us so we have to be careful."

"Yeah. We really shouldn't have him around here. He could get his ass in trouble. Send him home and keep checking up on him. Okay?"

"Yeah."

I went over to Joel, standing in front of the clubhouse bulletin board. He seemed to salivate over the shit the members posted for sale. An ad for a one of the member's selling a classic GTO had his attention.

"You can't afford it, kid," I said behind him.

He gave a pitiful shrug. "I know."

We both looked at it for a long time. "Nice car, though," I said. When he turned to look at me, I pointed to my watch. "You'd better get home for your warden."

He sniffed. "Can't. I got a text from the Fury. They want to meet me."

That didn't sound good. "You think they suspect anything?"

"Nah. They said they have a job they want me to do."

I checked my phone. It was ten-thirty. "Fine. But remember, you've got to be home by midnight. I promised your sister you wouldn't be late."

"Yeah. Okay."

I walked him to the door. "Keep doing what you're doing. I'll call you later. But at this point, it's not safe if you come around here anymore. Considering they're watching us."

He nodded. "Okay."

"All right. Get out of here. And be careful."

Joel gave me a wave and walked away. I watched him go outside and hop on his bike, all skinny angles that hadn't yet filled out. He sailed away, thank Christ, looking a little more competent with the bike than he had before. As he did, I shook my head and chuckled. He was probably the closest I'd ever come to having a little brother. Sure, there was Jet, but Jet had a massive chip on his shoulder and insisted on acting like an ass to make up for his lack of years.

This kid, Joel? He was crying for the help. Charlotte could only do so much. He needed a man to toughen him up. Show him how the world worked.

I wondered if I could be that person. In fact, it hadn't been all that shitty having him around my apartment, like I thought it would be. It was actually pretty cool.

But yeah, making him go to the clubhouse hadn't been the smartest thing I'd ever done. If Fury saw him here, they'd want his head on a platter.

If they did, I'd fall on the sword and tell them I'd dragged him here. But would I even get the chance?

Slade was gone, but that didn't mean the other guys weren't also ruthless assholes who'd fuck him up for consorting with us.

Yeah. I had to be careful. The next time we met, it'd have to be somewhere else.

I owed that to Charlotte, at least. I'd told her I'd protect him.

But she needed protection, too. Just as I'd promised Joel that if he fucked with us, we'd go after his family, the Fury had the same rule. Charlotte was in just as much danger.

Maybe more. At least Joel knew what he was up against. From what I'd heard, Charlotte was pretty much in the dark when it came to his prospecting for the Fury. Not to mention that he'd fucking mentioned his sister to them, when they'd called to ask him where he was.

She was on their radar.

Knowing the way the Fury operated, I could bet anything they'd already started watching her.

And she had no clue.

I'd only left her a couple of hours ago. But something made me want to see her again. I wanted to protect her. While Joel was up to his ass in shit for the Fury, he'd have to leave her by herself. I could catch her alone. Exactly the way I wanted her.

Alone, wet, and ready for me.

I slid on my bike, about to start the engine, when I remembered she was at work. Shit.

I searched for the location of the veterinarian on my phone. Luckily, this town only had one, a short ride away.

I jumped on the kick-start and headed off the pier away from the beach.

EVIE MONROE

Chapter Fourteen

Charlotte

It was unusual for me to find myself bored out of my head at work. Me, the consummate animal lover not loving the place right now. But that was how it went sometimes, especially when there was someplace else I'd rather be.

I rarely complained about work, though, but I didn't have the same job security as I once had. Business had fallen off. As much as the doctors liked me here, they'd gradually cut everyone's hours. I'd gone from full-time, when I started a couple of years ago, to part-time. I had good benefits, but I constantly worried what I'd do if they cut my hours anymore.

So that was probably why, as I sat at the receptionist stand, I started flipping through my phone, looking for part-time jobs to fill my extra hours.

The first one I saw? Albertson's. They needed cashiers. I laughed.

Oh, hell no.

Cashiering at Albertson's had been a good job. They liked me and would probably jump at a chance to have me back. But, I'd been happy to escape that place, and all the rumors about me that swirled around with it. It would be a step backwards.

Grumbling to myself, I closed out of the jobs website and checked my messages. Nothing from Jojo. It was nearly midnight and my shift ended soon. At that point, I'd text him to make sure he'd gotten home, as he promised.

I hoped Hart was having a good effect on him, and he'd actually stick to curfew this time.

As I was filing away some paperwork and clearing off the workspace for the next shift, Barb came in with two mugs of coffee. "I was about to fall asleep in the kitty litter. I made another cup. Hope you want one, too."

"Sure. Thanks," I said, accepting it gratefully.

She sat down next to me. "So, how's everything going with Jojo? He doing okay?"

Because we had so many techs on staff, Barb and I hadn't had one of our heart-to-hearts in a while. The last time I'd spoken to her, Joel had just started working his job at Jack in the Box but was exploring options for the next phase of his life. At least, that was what I told her. "Oh. Well. He's still trying to decide what he wants to do."

Barb smiled one of her never-ending smiles. I'd never seen her in a bad mood. "It's hard to make up your mind, of course. The rest of your life is an awfully long time."

Sure. I'd be happy if Jojo went short-term and just knew what he wanted to do this year, as long as it didn't involve anything illegal. "I guess."

"It's daunting."

I supposed so, but I never had a chance to be afraid. It was do or die for me. I had to get a job, or else. I wondered if Jojo would have risen to the challenge if he'd had that same pressure? By trying to provide a stable life where he could have a choice, was I actually doing him a disservice? "Sometimes I think I need to stick a cattle-prod under his butt, though."

She laughed. "Ah, that's the age. Our boys think video games and vegging are the be-all and end-all right now. Hopefully it's just a phase."

I sipped my coffee and agreed with her. Or let her think I did. Her son, Brandon, was a freshman at USC, so he obviously had taken a break from the video games long enough to study and get good grades. I couldn't say the same for Joel. What did she know about boys on the edge?

"How's Brandon doing?" I ventured, though I wasn't sure I wanted to know.

She didn't answer. Something she saw through the heavy glass double-doors up front caught her eye. The rare look of concern that flashed on her face made me think she'd seen the parking lot go up in flames. I followed her line of vision to see a rather large man.

On a motorcycle.

I jumped out of my chair, straining forward to make sure it wasn't a figment of my imagination. After all, my imagination had been rendering images of Hart ever since I'd left him that somebody should have labeled Not-Safe-For-Work.

But no, it wasn't a product of my imagination. He parked his bike in the lot, in what I believed was a handicap space. What a rebel. He was still straddling the bike.

He took off his helmet and shook his messy mop of hair into place, Barb said, "Looks like someone made a wrong turn. Think I should lock the door so he doesn't come in?"

My chair had rolled away a little, so when I went to sit back down on it, my ass hit the edge and I went down, my butt hitting the ground with a thud.

I looked up to see Barb peeking over the edge of the desk, eyes wide. "Are you okay?"

Before I could say anything, I heard the front door creak open and close, and a gruff voice said, "Charlotte here?"

I would've liked to spend the rest of my life under the desk, considering I had just taken a dive because of him. But why was he here? Had something happened to Jojo?

I jumped up like a jack in the box. "Here. Why? Is everything okay?"

He didn't necessarily look surprised. Amused, maybe. "What were you doing down there? Sleeping?"

I looked at Barb, who eyed me suspiciously. Though she was divorced, I knew a lot about her ex-husband and her current boyfriend, both clean-cut, tie-wearing, Silicon Valley executive types. Nothing like this man. She must've thought I'd gone off my rocker.

"No, I was just . . . searching for my earring back," I muttered, an obvious lie because I wasn't wearing earrings. "Why are you here again? Is Jojo okay?"

"Yeah. Last I checked an hour ago. He was fine."

"An hour ago? Why isn't he with you?"

"Because he said he had stuff to do, so I let him go, as long as he promised to be back home to you at midnight."

I sighed loudly. "Really? You just let him out of your sight like that?"

He looked at me like I was a fly on his sandwich. "Jesus, girl. Yeah."

I swear, his neck might have been a tree trunk, but I wanted to wrap my hands around it and shake him anyway. "What happened to looking after him?"

His eyes shifted to the side, and I realized Barb was watching this whole thing. I might have been friendly with Barb, but I didn't want her to see me blowing a gasket, not at work, which I was dangerously close to doing.

I needed to take Hart somewhere quiet to talk. I checked the clock. We had five minutes left on our shift.

Fine. I could hold my shit together for that long. He had five minutes left to live.

I clamped my mouth shut and decided I'd spend those five minutes getting my things together so I could run out the door and tear him a new asshole right at midnight. I finished cleaning off my workspace and when I looked up, Hart was extending his hand to Barb.

"Seeing as how Charlotte isn't going to introduce us . . . How are you doing? I'm Hart." He said it in a friendly way that made her smile and giggle like a schoolgirl.

Apparently his charm wasn't just for women my age.

"Charmed, Mr. Hart," she said, as I rolled my eyes. In what way was he a mister? "How do you know Charlotte?"

He said, very cordially, "I'm a friend of her brother's."

"Ah," Barb said. "It's very nice to meet you."

Since they were getting along so well, I went to the locker and grabbed my purse. When I returned, the next shift had arrived and something had Barb laughing hysterically. She bent over nearly in half and slapped her knee snickering about some joke of Hart's. What the fuck? Nothing he'd said so far had ever been that funny to me.

When I cleared my throat, they looked at me as if I'd interrupted them. I said to Barb, "Mind if I bow out a minute early, Barb? I've got to check on my brother." I shot a couple of daggers in Hart's direction.

"No, no, of course!" she sang. "It was nice meeting you, Mr. Hart!"

The last I saw, he gave her a wink. I threw open the door and let it go as quickly as I passed through it, so it'd slam in his face if he followed me.

Which he did. A second later, he was right behind me, his hand on my shoulder, so I spun on him. "Get away from me."

He dropped his hands. "What? You're telling me your pissed because I didn't follow your brother around with TP so I could wipe his ass?"

"No. I'm pissed because you promised you'd look after him and now he's not with you. Do you even know where he is?"

"Yeah. He went to his club. But he promised he'd be back by midnight."

I pulled my keys out of my purse. "I wouldn't put too much faith in his promises if I were you."

"Jesus Christ, Charlie. For the last time, he's an adult. You have to loosen the leash. When I was his age, I was on my own."

"I've been on my own all my goddamn life!" I shot back at him. "The difference is, I can handle it. He can't. You don't know him, Hart. You don't know anything!"

He dug his hands into his pockets and started to stalk away, his back tense.

When he turned around, I tore open the door to my car and said, "And if you call me Charlie one more time, I'll fuck you up!" and slammed the door to the car before he could say whatever insults were on his tongue.

I felt good, for about ten seconds, as I sped out of the parking lot. Didn't even care that I punched the gas and my tires squealed just as Barb was walking into the lot. But as he disappeared from my rear-view mirror, I started to feel worse and worse.

Why was he such a dumbass?

Why did I think I could rely on such a dumbass?

And why, even though I knew he was a dumbass, was every pore in my body wanting him again?

By the time I got back to the apartment, I'd already cursed Hart's name in every way imaginable. Who did he think he was, showing up at my place of employment? What did he think he was doing, leaving Jojo when I expressly told him not to? And why did he have to be so goddamn fucking hot?

I neared my parking space, and—no surprise—that bike that Jojo had been tooling around in lately was nowhere to be seen. I pressed my lips together smugly as a second later, Hart sailed into the empty space beside me.

"See?" I said, jumping out of the car. I held out my phone to him. "It's twelve-fifteen. You see how well he keeps his promises? This is why I can't treat him like an adult!"

Hart cut the engine on his bike and took off his helmet. "Give him a few minutes. He'll be here."

I was already jabbing an incoherent text to Jojo's phone, telling him I was going to kill him, in all caps, with lots of punctuation. "Fuck that. I've given him enough free passes. You have no idea."

I expected an argument, but when I looked up, he was nodding. Amazing. He didn't have a response.

"I'm going inside," I muttered, pressing SEND on the text and heading up the path to my apartment.

He followed me. "Want me to take my bike out and look for him?"

"No. I don't. You've done enough. Just go," I said, walking faster, my head down.

Hart didn't give up. He followed me. As I ran up the stairs, I saw a light on in our apartment window. I'd left quickly, so I might have left it on, or . . . maybe Jojo had come back. Maybe his crap cycle had given out on him and he'd had to get rid of it. A little flash of hope ignited in me.

Eager to see, I knocked, then fiddled with the key, trying to get the door open as the dogs began to yip inside.

But when I threw open the door, I looked around and saw everything just the way I'd left it. I must've just forgotten to turn the light off.

I fisted both hands, stalked to the sofa, pulled up a pillow, and punched it with a loud "Ahhhhh!"

"Hey. Calm down."

I looked back at the door. Hart stood there, looking at me with an expression that said, *aren't you overreacting again?* I took the pillow and chucked it at him, hard.

He calmly caught it as Opie dashed between his legs. Talk about making everything worse. I didn't need calm. I needed someone to be as riled up and outraged over this as I was.

"What the fuck are you doing here?" I snarled. "You've done enough. Get out of my apartment!"

His look turned to downright incredulous. "Are you fucking serious? I came here to check on you. To make sure you're all right. And this is the thanks I get?"

Okay, I wasn't going to cave that easily, like a piece of wilted lettuce. I stalked up to him. "No one asked you to. I asked you to watch over my brother, which you clearly can't do. And . . ." I stopped as something hit me. "Why would you think I wouldn't be all right?"

He shrugged his shoulder. Was there something he wasn't telling me?

Oh, fuck. If he wasn't telling me something, I'd beat it out of him. If Jojo was in bigger trouble than Hart was letting on. If he thought he was protecting me by keeping me in the dark . . . he had another think coming. "What . . . what the fuck does that mean? What's going on?"

He stared down at me with those light, intoxicating eyes that were my total undoing, as I tried not to crack.

"Hart. Tell me. If you know something . . ."

He didn't have to tell me shit. He knew he had me. Damn him. He knew all he had to do was stand there, and I'd drop my panties for him and do his bidding.

"Goddammit." I raised my fists to him and started to pummel his chest. I didn't care. I'd beat it out of him if this was the way he wanted to play it.

He let me. For a good ten seconds, he let me lay into him. I doubt it hurt him because he didn't take a step back or block me or anything. He just let me use him as my whipping post.

Then suddenly and fiercely, he grabbed both my wrists. It was so unexpected, I let out a gasp. He held them tight, in between us.

"Don't," he said, his voice low and rumbling.

I'd had men hold me like that before. Usually, foster fathers, right before they beat my ass, or threw me across the room. I held my breath in anticipation of the pain.

Instead, he pulled me up to him and our mouths crashed together.

He let go of my wrists as his tongue controlled my mouth, his powerful hands reached around me and grabbed my ass. The second he did, I felt the wetness between my legs, my pussy so achy for him, wanting him so much I could barely stand, even with him holding me up. His body pressed against mine, and I responded, my nipples painfully hard against his chest.

Coherent thought went out the window. My senses took over. God, his smell was delicious, and the taste of him even more so. The feel of his stubble against my face was painfully addictive. That was what it was, all pain and pleasure and so much need. I couldn't even remember what I'd been so angry about.

Yes! Yes! More! I thought as his tongue plundered my mouth and his hands massaged my ass. I ran my hands around his back, lifting his shirt.

He didn't lift me and take me to the bed this time. No, this time he walked me toward the couch. As he did, he reached for the hem of my scrubs shirt, then his warm hands dove underneath, molding my breasts through my bra as he kissed me, groaning and licking at my lips.

He broke the kiss and gazed into my eyes, pressing his forehead against mine. "I want to fuck you again."

I nodded, the bobble-head nod. Again. I wanted that, too. Really, what had I been so angry about, before? Blinded by need, I reached down, grabbed the hem of my shirt, and pulled it up over my head, shaking my ponytail free. "Good. I want that too. I want to feel you inside me."

I guessed I must have been so out-of-it that not only had I forgotten my brother, I'd gone deaf to the roaring sound of his motorcycle. Because the second I told Hart to fuck me, the door swung open and Jojo walked in saying, "Sorry I'm—"

Hart and I broke apart like two magnets of the same charge, and I clasped my shirt over my breasts. Jojo stopped, his eyes trailing from Hart's face to my shocked expression and turned on his heel.

"Fuck you both," he called over his shoulder as his boots hammered their way down the stairs outside.

Eyes wide, I looked at Hart, who wasn't looking at me. He'd already started to race after Jojo.

I covered my mouth with my hands as realization set in. What the fuck was I doing?

For the first time, my little brother had totally slipped my mind. How could I have let go of a piece of my heart like that so easily? If anyone had asked me a week ago if that could ever happen, I'd have told them they were insane.

Turned out all it took was one hot, badass motorcycle man to make me forget everything I thought I knew.

Chapter Fifteen

Hart

I didn't have to be a genius to know that Charlie was mortified. So I did the only thing I could do. I turned tail and chased after her brother.

My cock was hard as a rock by then, so I adjusted it in my pants as I tore after him. He was a fast little thing. I didn't catch up with him until he'd reached his bike, and even then, I had to call after him.

"Wait. Joel. Chill out for a second," I said as I reached the curb.

"Fuck you. I don't have to listen to you anymore. You're a fucking asshole."

He jumped on his bike, but I reached for the keys and twisted them out of his hand before he could stick them in the ignition. He made a grab for them, but I yanked them away and backed up to the curb. "Come on. Just listen to me."

He scowled at me, breathing hard. "Why the fuck should I? Is that what you were planning, this whole time? To fuck my sister? Is that why you're doing all this?"

I shook my head. "You know that's not true. I didn't even know you had a sister until yesterday."

He blew out a breath of air. "Yeah. You wasted no time trying to get in her pants."

"Hey. Sorry to break it to you, kid, but I didn't really have to try that hard."

In retrospect, that was the wrong thing to say. He pushed off his bike and came at me, fists clenched. He got off one punch, barely connecting with my shoulder before I grabbed his hand. I wrenched him around, twisting his arm behind his back, and shoved him to the ground so I was standing over him. He fought me, but I had at least fifty pounds on the kid, and a shit ton more muscle. There was no match.

I didn't want to have the kid sprawled out on his stomach on the concrete, cheek against the ground, arm bent up behind him, but he left me no choice. He wiggled to get free as I gritted out. "If you calm down so we can talk about this, I'll let you go."

He spit on my boot. "Go to fucking hell."

I let go of him anyway, just because I deserved it. I'd have probably been pissed off too if someone was trying to fuck my sister. Good thing I didn't have one.

He pushed up onto his knees, then staggered to his feet and shoved my chest with both hands. "You fucker! You fucking disgusting motherfucking piece of shit!"

I pushed him back, just once, not hard, but firmly, and he staggered a few steps backwards, whatever rage in his eyes melting away to defeat. Oh, the hate was still there, but at least he'd learned not to mess with me.

He held a finger up, in defensive position, like I was the one attacking him, even though everything I'd done so far was in self-defense. "Listen to me, fucker. Hear this loud and clear. Get the fuck out of here, and don't come back. You, and all of the Cobra pieces of shit. You all can stay away from me and my sister."

"You said you didn't like your sister messing in your business. Well, maybe you should stay out of hers," I said calmly.

"You *are* my business," he seethed, his fists closing again as he raised them to chest level. I stood there, braced for the onslaught, but he didn't come at me. "I don't know. I thought we were . . . I thought you were my . . ."

He stopped, and his face trembled a little, like he might break down.

Before he could, I said, "Look. I am your friend. Okay? But that has nothing to do with Charlie."

"What the . . . *Charlie?*" He paced away from me, then rounded back. "What the fuck? So how long have you and *Charlie* been fucking? You get her into bed the second you met her? That's how you guys operate, right? The more women, the better. I should've fucking known."

"It's not like that, kid. Listen, I got to thinking about the way the Fury operates, and if they get wind that you're dealing with us, they'd fuck you up. You made a mistake when you told them all about her. So I went to her job to check on her, and it just happened."

His lips turned up into a snarl. "*It just happened,*" he mocked. "I don't believe that shit. My sister doesn't need anyone looking after her, least of all, you. She's tough. She can hold her own."

I shook my head. "No. If the Fury sees her as a threat, there's no telling what they'd do. She can't defend herself against them, and you can't defend her, either. They'd kill you and kill her . . . or worse. Put her on the street to make them money and own her." I crossed my arms. "Is that what you want?"

"You're lying," he said, his voice cracking.

"No. I've seen it before. That's the way they treat women. They nearly killed Drake's girl, Cait. Cait is Slade's daughter. If Slade nearly killed Cait and her mom, the Fury'd think nothing of killing your sister."

He scoffed, until he realized I was dead serious. "You mean it?"

I nodded.

"And the Cobras treat their women better?"

"Yeah. That might be how the Fury works, but that ain't how we work," I said to him. "And Charlie's different. I like her."

He raised an eyebrow. "Oh, you *like* her? So that makes it all right." He blew out a breath of air, raked both hands through his hair, and crouched on the grass, staring at the ground. "Jesus. You better do a hell of a lot more than that, asshole."

"She's not just some girl to me. And regardless of what you think about the Fury, I don't fuck around. I'm not going to fuck her over, if that's what you mean."

"Oh, you'd better not. I'll fuck you up. If you hurt her, I'll kill you."

I doubted that, but point taken. After all this, I had to admit, I was actually starting to like the kid. He didn't fit in with the Fury, not one fucking bit. The way he was willing to protect his sister? To me, he seemed like a Cobra, all the way.

I lifted my hands in surrender. "If I ever do hurt her, I'll let you."

He pressed his lips together, thinking. "After all this time she's spent trying to warn me away from guys like you . . ." He let out a sour laugh. "It figures. It figures she'd fall for one of you. You understand, she doesn't do this, normally."

I was glad he sounded a little more rational. "What do you mean?"

"She doesn't date. She doesn't even talk to guys. She's like a fucking saint. I used to think she was a nun in another life." He leaned over and picked at a blade of grass . "So she must really like you. Just . . . really. I meant what I said. She's the best person I know. Hands down."

"I got it."

He shook his head. "I don't think you do. I don't think you can, unless you know . . ." He trailed off, and his eyes clouded over. "Doesn't matter. Just . . . you've been warned. I'm a shit to her, I know. But if you don't put her on a pedestal where she belongs, fuck you."

It did seem hypocritical for him to give me these warnings when he hadn't treated her so great lately. But I ignored it. I reached my hand out to him to help him up.

He stared at it for a long time, as if deciding whether or not to take it.

"What would you say if I told you I wanted you to be a Cobra?" I asked him.

His eyes widened for a split second before narrowing in suspicion. "Why? That because you feel guilty for fucking my sister?"

I shook my head. "It's because I think you're one of us. Not one of them. I'll sponsor you, if you want."

He opened his mouth, but nothing came out, and when he closed it, the corner lifted up into a smile. "Yeah?" He grabbed hold of my hand and I pulled him to his feet. "Then all right."

"Good. I'll get you all the info you need to get on board with us, okay?"

"But . . ." His eyes drifted toward the apartment complex. I was sure Charlotte had her eyes on us, but in the darkness all I could see was the light in the window. "What about the Fury? Won't they be pissed?"

I nodded. Pissed was the understatement of the year. "Oh yeah."

He kept his eyes on the apartment. "I don't know . . . maybe Charlotte's right. What if they find out? I don't care about me . . . but what about her? I can't have anything happen to her."

We walked toward the apartment. As much as I wanted to be with Charlie, I'd made the decision that I wouldn't go back inside, just for the kid's sake. He'd been through enough. "You don't need to figure it out tonight."

He stared at the ground. "I don't know. I'm fucking up where Char's concerned. What I need to do is get a good job. Something to help her pay the bills. Make it easier on her."

"Well . . . we're looking for a guy at the garage. You know anything about oil changes?"

"Yeah. A little."

"It's mostly just keeping the place clean. The pay's shit. But it's a good way to start."

He considered it. "Yeah. Thanks. I might be interested."

"Look," I said to him. "If you're seriously in to this, and the guys agree, you have the Cobra's word that we'll protect you. All right?"

He nodded, but something in his expression said he wasn't sure.

"Just trust me, okay?" I said, clapping him on the back. "Go inside, get some sleep. I'll text you later. Just keep doing what you're doing with the Fury in the meantime. All right?"

"Yeah. Okay. Thanks."

"Everything go okay with them, tonight?"

He nodded. "I don't think they suspect anything."

"Good."

As I got back on my bike, saw Joel jogging up the steps to his apartment. I wished I was a fly on the wall to hear the conversation he had with his sister, but I figured I was already skating on some pretty thin ice as it was.

So I strapped on my helmet, started my bike, and lit out of the parking lot toward my place.

EVIE MONROE

Chapter Sixteen

Charlotte

After I got over the stunned feeling of shame over what I'd just done, my thoughts automatically turned to making sure my brother was okay.

I pulled on my shirt, ran for the door, then heard him unleashing a string of curses into the night air. Curses meant not just for Hart, but for me, as well.

I crept over to the balcony and looked over the rail. Hart had him on his stomach, on the ground, trying to subdue him, but the second Hart let him go, Jojo was up again, shoving him. Again, Hart stopped it, but that didn't stop Jojo from shouting at him, calling him a motherfucker.

Hart spoke so calmly; I could barely hear him. As I strained to listen, doors on either side of me opened and people started looking out. It was after one in the morning.

One of my neighbors, a fifty-something man who lived alone and spent most of his time with a bottle of beer in his hand, slurred, "What the fuck's going on here, for *fucksake*?"

"Nothing," I explained as he looked over the balcony. "Just some guys talking."

He looked me over, head to toe, winked at me, and went back inside, slamming the door.

By then, Jojo had crouched down on the grass to listen calmly to Hart. He nodded his head like he understood. I couldn't hear most of it, but I heard Jojo say, "If you don't put her on a pedestal where she belongs, fuck you."

My heart squeezed. There was the little brother I knew and loved.

I moved closer, wanting to hear Hart's answer, but I couldn't. I wanted to hear more of what Hart thought of me, and what we were doing here. I mean, we barely knew each other. Of course it was just sex. But with my little brother involved, it was complicated. Clearly, he respected Hart. And Hart didn't seem all that terrible a person anymore.

Jojo and I were both starting to fall a little bit in love with Hart. Which would make it doubly hard for Jojo, if the relationship went south. I could probably deal with it, but for the first time I'd found a guy that Jojo could look up to. And I didn't want to ruin that.

I listened as Hart offered to sponsor my brother as part of his club. I thought he'd jump at the chance. I thought I'd have the urge to go out there and tell Hart to take his invitation and shove it up his ass.

But something strange happened. I found myself glad that Hart made the offer to sponsor him, to be the big brother he never had. It was Jojo who hesitated.

He shook his head and looked up toward the apartment. Something was bothering him. I wasn't sure what it was, but when he mentioned the other motorcycle club, it hit me just why Hart had come over here.

If Jojo broke his promise to pledge a different club, and went with Hart's club, there'd likely be hard feelings. Or maybe something more than that.

Were we in danger?

Hart helped Jojo off the ground and headed to his bike. I was glad of that, even though all the while, my body still ached for him. I needed to talk to Jojo first. Explain myself.

After Hart's motorcycle roared into the distance, Jojo came climbing up the staircase. I tried to make myself busy, cleaning out the litter boxes. When he appeared in the doorway, I met his eyes. He looked tired and beaten. He crossed the room and sat on the sofa, and Opie crawled into his lap. He didn't say anything for a long time.

Finally, he said, "Well. He's not an asshole."

I supposed that was as much of a blessing as I could expect from him. "I didn't mean for it to happen, Jo—" I swallowed back his nickname. "Joel. I swear, I thought I hated him. But he's been so good with you, and he's the first guy that's really been nice to us. I just—I just like him. Is that so bad?"

He shook his head. "You don't have to explain it, Char. You don't owe me anything."

I wasn't so sure about that. After the life he'd had, I felt like the world owed him some sense of stability and security. But the world was never going to pay up, so as the person closest to him, I'd have to take its place. I replaced the litter box and sat on the coffee table, across from him. "You're not mad at me?"

It took him a while, but eventually the corner of his mouth quirked up into a smile. "I kind of am."

I tweaked his knee, like I used to when he was a kid. "So, baby brother. Are you going to tell me what's going on? With these two motorcycle clubs?"

He yawned and started to shuffle in his seat, preparing to get up. "Aw, Char, I—"

I lunged toward him, took hold of his shoulders, and pushed him back down onto the sofa with all my weight. He nudged me off of him, but I ended up in corralling him on the couch so he couldn't move. "Don't tell me you're too tired. What's going on? Are you, like, working as a spy against the other club or what?"

He hung his head lower and nodded.

"Tell me," I urged. "Everything."

He let out an enormous sigh. "Fine. The Cobras—that's Hart's club—saw that I was a prospect for the Hell's Fury, and they took me in. They were making me act like a spy for them, yeah. But the two clubs are in a war and the Fury doesn't play so nice." He rolled his eyes, like he was worried, or worse. "Hart offered to sponsor me as a prospect for the Cobras but if I do that, I'm in deep shit with the Fury. And Hart doesn't want them coming after me. Or you."

I blinked. My heart stopped. My eyes immediately went to the door. Had Joel locked it? "They would do that?"

"Supposedly, yeah."

"All of this, to join a stupid motorcycle club?"

"Yeah."

I threw up my hands. "Great, Jojo. Tell me why joining a club was so important to you, now?"

"I don't know!" he said, his voice so loud and broken that it cracked. "I guess it was a stupid fucking idea. I want brothers. Brothers like the Cobras have. They all have each other's backs. They get together and they rely on each other and they're . . . *family*."

"*I'm* your family," I said softly. Then I reached over and tried to ruffle his hair, but he flinched away. "But I know. I know you want more than that. You want what I can't be for you."

He swallowed. "You're not so bad."

I smiled a little. "Well . . . what if we left Aveline Bay? What if we just moved away? Went somewhere no one could find us?"

"Yeah. I hear there's a private island off the coast of Fiji we could hide out in." He snorted. "With what money?"

I lifted my shoulders in an attempt at optimism. "I don't know. We'd figure it out. We always have, haven't we?"

"Yeah. But it just means starting over again from scratch. Hart told me he could probably get me a job at the garage. We have connections here. You have a good job."

That was true. Hart had Jojo thinking about a job, now? It was a big step up, considering only a few days ago I saw him as nothing but a lazy ass. I also hated the idea of uprooting us. Still, it could be worse.

I laced my hands in front of me and looked at my lap. "Jojo . . . I mean, Joel . . .I'd rather live out of our car than for you to get hurt."

He laughed. "Yeah, we could live in a car, with all your pets. We could be a traveling zoo."

I smacked him. "I mean it, Jojo. I couldn't take it if I lost you. I really couldn't."

This time, he reached over and touched my arm. "You won't. Hart said the Cobras protect their own. I trust him."

I was afraid to admit it, because that was usually when the floor dropped out from under us, but I trusted him, too. I barely knew him, but he made good on his promises, which was more than most people in our lives had done.

"All right," I said to him, checking the clock again. I cringed at the late hour. "I guess we should go to bed."

I went off to my room, feeling good about things with Jojo, despite how disastrous I feared they'd be. But I didn't like the can of worms we'd opened with these rival motorcycle clubs. It kept me awake all night, wondering how much danger we were really in.

I could understand why Jojo found the Cobras and that brotherhood so attractive, but still . . . that wasn't him. He was a sensitive kid, a good one. He might have seen Hart as the kind of guy he aspired to be, but this life wasn't something he'd bargained for.

Jojo couldn't handle the kind of danger he'd fallen into. He wasn't cut from the same cloth as people like Hart.

By morning, I knew I needed to talk to Hart, as soon as possible. I needed to see what he could do to keep my brother and me safe.

Chapter Seventeen

Hart

I decided to give them both some space.

Not that I didn't keep a watch on them. But based on what I heard from the other Cobras, with the Fury, it was business as usual. Based on the intel I pulled from Joel's phone, Fury didn't have a clue that Joel was talking to us. It seemed like we were in the clear.

So I figured it was a good idea to cool it with Charlie for the next few days. Not that I didn't think about her.

And I guessed they were thinking about me, too. About the same time I got a text from Joel, telling me he had intel on the Fury, I got another text from Charlie. It said: *Are you avoiding us?*

I'd been at the Lucky Leaf, helping Nix on an engine rebuild. Wiping the grease off my hands on an old rag, I typed in: *Just thought it was better to cool it. For your sake.*

A moment later, she responded with: *Well, don't. I need to talk to you.*

As I was staring at my phone, Nix nudged me. We'd finished up for the day and we'd planned on going to The Wall with Jet for a beer. "Hey. You coming?"

I pointed at my phone. "I'll be there later. Our kid might have some info."

Nix raised an eyebrow. "Want me to come with?"

I shook my head. We'd taken too many risks, having the kid at the clubhouse and also my apartment. I'd made the decision to meet with him somewhere outside of town. Outside of town would take a while to get to, since Aveline Bay wasn't exactly a small town. I'd have to cross the bridge and head north. "Better if I do this myself."

"Suit yourself. We'll see you later," he called over his shoulder. He strapped on his helmet and rode off on his bike.

As much as I wanted to see Charlie, she'd have to wait. I couldn't just show up at her apartment. After my conversation with Joel, I felt the burning need to keep her safe. I texted Joel and told him to meet me under the bridge of the highway, outside of town. It was the most remote place I could think of.

About forty minutes later, I pulled off the highway and rolled to a stop under the bridge. I spotted Joel waiting for me, still wearing his denim kutte with the Hell's Fury prospect patch on it, smoking a cigarette, which he stubbed out when I got there.

"What's going on?" I asked him, sitting back on my bike as I unstrapped my helmet. "You think they know anything?"

He shook his head. "No fucking way. The Fury's a mess right now. Bruiser's been dead a while, and now with Slade gone, too, they're missing their president and their Veep. It's chaos. They're all fighting for who should take the reins. A fistfight broke out in the clubhouse yesterday, which turned into a knife fight. There was blood all over the place."

"Jesus," I laughed. "So who do you think it's gonna be?"

"Probably Scar. He's got most of the support, and he's been there the longest. But who knows? All I know is that it's not a good place to be right now. Total disorganization."

I rubbed the stubble on my chin. "So they're not after you, now?"

"Nah. They didn't even pay attention to me."

"So they're probably not after us, either, then." I was thinking out loud.

"Yeah. They got bigger fish to fry."

"But eventually, they'll come after us," I said, tilting my head up, then slipping off my sunglasses and staring at him. "So we can't let our guard down. Keep watching your back, kid. All right?"

He nodded. "Right. So, did you talk to the guys about me joining?"

I had. The guys had been all for it, and of course, Jet had acted like it was all his idea, even though he hadn't lifted a pinky finger. The only one who wasn't sure was Nix, but that was because he'd nearly taken a bullet from him.

"So, yeah," I said, "If you want to do it . . ."

"I do." He sounded more eager now. More sure of himself.

"Well, we're all in on you becoming a prospect. We just might want to wait a little bit until things are over with the Fury, if you know what I mean. Because even if they're in disarray, if you turn up suddenly wearing our patch, you probably ain't gonna be seeing home again."

"Yeah. Makes sense. But when'll that be?"

I shrugged. "No clue. I'm gonna talk to Cullen. I think right now we have enough intel, so you won't have to keep playing both sides. So if he agrees, we keep you the fuck away from them until we get things settled."

He nodded coolly, but a stiff breeze rushed under the bridge right then, making him shudder. He steeled himself and reached into the pocket of his kutte for another cigarette. I reached for my own and lit his and mine with my lighter.

"Sounds good," he said, his voice lighter as if maybe he'd been worried I'd change my mind. "But what about Char?"

"Keep an eye on your sister. As much as you can."

"And you?"

He was testing me. "Yeah. I will, too. The Cobras protect all the families, and that goes for her, too."

"No. I mean, have you called her. Since that night?" he asked. "Because I can tell. She's getting anxious. She thinks you're blowing her off. That better not be the case."

I rolled my eyes to the sky. "It's not, as a matter of fact. I plan to call your sister after this meeting." I raised an eyebrow at him. "As long as you're okay with it?"

He looked kinda helpless when he said, "Don't think I have a choice."

"You do. I'm sure if you told her you didn't want her seeing me anymore, I'd have to believe she'd probably do what you told her."

He smirked. "And if she kicked you to the curb, you'd kick my ass. I know how that works."

"First thing you need to know if you're gonna be a Cobra," I said, laughing, "is that we aren't too fond of kicking our brother's asses."

The smirk became a smile. A real one, the first I'd seen on the kid since I met him. He was about to say something when he stopped and lifted his phone out of his pocket, checking the display. "Shit. It's Scar," he said, his voice small.

"Answer it," I directed.

He put the phone to his ear. "Hey man . . ." he said, speaking in a stilted, nervous tone, the way he'd spoken to me, before he'd gotten more comfortable. "Yeah. Yeah. Okay. I can be there. Give me twenty."

He hung up the phone, a look of dread on his face.

"Fuck me," he muttered, trying to stick the phone back in his pocket. He missed the first try. "FUCK. ME."

"They need you?"

He nodded. "Yeah. To help out with some of their bikes, or something. I've got to go to their clubhouse."

"All right."

He walked to his bike like his boots were made of lead. "Have fun with my sister," he said. I couldn't tell if he was teasing me or if he really meant it.

Then he took off. I finished my cigarette, stubbed it out on the ground, and followed the way he'd gone about five minutes later, heading south, back into Aveline Bay.

I had a girl I couldn't wait to see.

Chapter Eighteen

Charlotte

Two days after I last saw Hart, I was going fucking insane.

It wasn't anything new to me. I'd met guys, gone crazy over them, only to have them drop off the face of the earth. The thing was, Hart didn't seem like that kind of guy.

I got the feeling he was keeping a respectful distance because of Jojo, and I got confirmation of that after I finally bit the bullet and texted him. After that, I told him I really needed to speak to him.

Then, no answer.

He may have been trustworthy and loyal, but he knew how to play infuriating mind games like all the other guys.

It was nearly nine, and the vet hadn't given me any hours until the weekend, so I was sitting in bed, watching mindless reality television and wondering how I was going to make rent, when my phone buzzed. I was hoping for a message from Jojo, since he'd left a few hours before, *to see friends*, he'd said. I wasn't sure what that meant.

But instead, I saw Hart's name on the display.

I rocketed up in my bed and read the message. *Can you meet me?*

I looked across the room, at my reflection in the mirror above the dresser. In the greenish glow of the television, I had quite the zombie-ish appearance. I smoothed down my flyaway hair and wiped at my cheeks, then typed in: *Where?*

I licked my lips, waiting for a response. *You know where Green Grove Park is?*

Of course I knew Green Grove Park, a ten-minute walk from me, but not much of a park anymore. Heavily wooded and behind a housing development, it was home to a dilapidated metal swing set and a bunch of really old grills and camping sites. Always empty of picnickers, now, most of the time it was where kids went to get high.

I figured he must really be worried about the other motorcycle club seeing us together if he wanted to meet there. I typed in: *Y.*

Picnic tables. Fifteen minutes.

He sounded so very authoritative, I had to wonder if he was used to ordering people around and getting them to do his bidding. I'd only known him for a few days, and yet, he had me jumping when he said jump.

Heart pounding in my chest, I sprang out of bed. In a flash I'd slipped into denim shorts and a tank top, stuck my hair in a messy bun, blushed my cheeks and glossed my lips, even though we were meeting in the dark.

Didn't matter. I couldn't wait to see him.

Oh, yeah. And talk about how to protect Jojo. On my way out the door, I looked at my phone and realized that in my excitement, I'd missed a text from Jojo. It said: *I'll be home around eleven.*

I smiled and checked the time. Two more hours. At least something Hart had said to him had clicked. Still, I had to wonder, if he wasn't with Hart . . . what was he doing? Was he with that other club? I hated thinking of him lying to them, digging himself deeper into trouble.

I locked up the apartment and walked to the main road, headed for the park, telling myself that I needed to concentrate on getting Jojo out of the MC mess he'd gotten himself into. I steeled myself to be good and do my best to ignore Hart's muscular body, his low, sexy voice that seemed to vibrate deep inside me, the delicious way he smelled.

Jojo. Saving Jojo. That was the important thing.

I'd forgotten once before, and it had led to the most embarrassing situation of my life. If Jojo had walked in five minutes later, things would've been even worse.

I swallowed hard, trying to steel myself when I came to an asphalt path, barred by a metal gate to keep cars from entering. A sign said, *Green Grove Park*

Open from Sunrise to Sunset, but it was so faded by the sun and obscured by tree branches, it was barely visible.

I knew this park well, because when I was a kid, one of my foster parents had enrolled me in a summer camp here. In the dark, though, it looked like a completely different place. As I walked away from the glow of the streetlamps, I found myself in almost perfect blackness.

I knew the general direction of the picnic tables but was pretty sure I wouldn't find them until I ran straight into one. I fanned my hands out and walked slowly into the depths of the park. Somewhere above, an owl hooted.

It occurred to me that this was damn stupid. Here I was, about to meet a strange guy in the middle of a dark, deserted place, without any backup. This was a recipe for trouble.

The thought didn't stop me, though. I guess I wanted trouble. I slowed when, in the distance, I saw the tiny fiery tip of a cigarette. A small shaft of moonlight filtered through the trees overhead, illuminating the chrome handlebars of a motorcycle. I took in a shaky breath. "Hart?"

A moment later, my eyes adjusted to the minimal light, and I saw him, motioning for me. He was sitting on the top of one of the picnic tables, smoking a cigarette. "Yeah. Come here."

I did, careful not to trip over a tree root or the crumbling asphalt of the pathway. As I did, I looked around and rubbed my arms. It was a lot chillier here than I'd expected.

Before I could get much closer, Hart flicked the cigarette away and reached out, snaked a hand around my waist, and pulled me to him. I smelled the scent of his cigarette, mingling with his own delicious aftershave, and as much as I wanted to melt into him, I stiffened. "That's not what I came here for."

It didn't stop him. He dipped his head and buried it in my neck, smelling me, then he delivered feather-like kisses to my collarbone. "It's okay," he said, his breath warm on my cool skin and so inviting. "It's what *I* came here for."

I couldn't stop him. It felt too good. I tilted my head back to the moon to give him better access and leaned in to him. "Why didn't you call me?"

His voice was muffled against my skin. "Told you. I wanted to make sure Joel was okay with this."

He trailed his lips up the side of my neck, took my earlobe into his mouth, and sucked, tonguing it gently. I inhaled deeply, before I lost all train of thought. "But . . .he told me you wanted him to join your club."

"Mmm-hmm," he growled out. With one hand he pushed my hair back, the other had gone under my tank top and to caress the small of my back. I stood between his legs, my hands on each strong thigh. I could feel his hardening cock against my stomach.

"But I don't want that," I said.

He ignored me and just kept nuzzling my neck, sucking on my ear, slowly undoing me. Soon I wouldn't even know my own name.

"Hart. Stop," I said. He didn't. I put both hands on his chest and pushed away. "Listen to me. Stop."

I couldn't see his face in the darkness, but I sensed his body tense, and he let out a groan of disappointment. "What? I thought you were gonna let the kid make his own decisions."

I swallowed. "I don't think you understand. Yes, he wants to be like you. But he isn't like you. He's afraid."

He let out a breath. "You don't think I wasn't afraid when I prospected, too? He just needs to grow some balls."

"No, he doesn't!" I fired back. "He's had enough trauma in his life. Trauma from being tossed around from place to place. No one to care for him. No one to love him. Maybe for once in his life it'd be nice to have some stability, don't you think? That's what I've been trying to give him."

His voice was low. "And you? What did you have?"

I didn't want to go into my sad story, which was probably worse than my brother's. I just shook my head. "He's not equipped for this life. And I really worry that being in between clubs is going to take a toll on him."

"Is that what he said?"

I nodded. "I talked to him the other night. He wants to be a part of something. And he likes you and wants to make you happy. But he's afraid if he turns down your invitation, you'll turn your back on him."

"He said that?"

"He didn't have to. I can tell. I know him, Hart."

He was silent for a long moment. "So what are you saying?"

"I'm saying that if there isn't any way to get out of this web he's tangled himself up in, then I'm going to take him out of the city. He doesn't think we can possibly make it with no money and no support, but if he's in danger, then we have to go."

"No, you don't. If he's a Cobra, we'll protect him."

"But he's not a Cobra. He's playing tough around you but he's not you. He's not some guy who likes to go around causing trouble and being all gangster. He's a good kid, Hart."

He came back right away, his voice hard-edged. "What do you mean? That's not what the Cobras are, Charlie. Maybe the Fury was, but we ain't the Fury."

"But . . ." I stammered, feeling him draw me closer. I knew he was looking at me, and even though I could see very little, I couldn't raise my eyes up to his.

I felt his hands come around me, digging into the pockets of my shorts and caressing my ass. "You know me, right? Am I really such a bad guy?"

"No," I admitted. "You're not. But I don't care. I can't do this. I need him out of this life completely."

"You can't force him."

I laughed sadly. "You know I can. Yes, he might be pissed for a while and give me crap, but eventually he'll feel guilty, and he'll do what I tell him to do. He always does. That's what tells me he's still has some of that good kid left in him. And I'm not going to give up on him yet."

He pulled his hands out of my pockets and straightened. "So that's it? You're leaving."

"Yeah. I think I have to."

"And I think you're making a mistake."

I was glad it was dark. Because if I'd seen those light hazel eyes of his, those eyes that made me do the things I never thought I could do, I knew I'd be a goner. "But what you think," I said, "doesn't matter."

EVIE MONROE

Chapter Nineteen

Hart

Charlie was as pig-headed as they came. Which only made me want her more. She was talking some ridiculous shit about taking her brother and hitting the road, leaving Aveline Bay altogether. How did she think that was going to help her situation?

"What I think doesn't matter?" I challenged. "Really?"

"Yes. I have to do what's best for my family."

"Joel's going to fight you."

"I know. But eventually he'll come around. So that's why I wanted to talk to you. I want you to stop encouraging him about this Cobras stuff. I want you to tell him that I'm right. That you think the best decision is for us to leave. If we're both telling him the same thing, he'll listen."

I let out a laugh. "Are you kidding me? That's not the best decision. Not by a long shot."

Her voice went sour. "Why? You think cruising around here, waiting to be shot is better?"

"No. It just ain't that simple."

"Oh? Why not? It's got to be simpler than staying around here as target practice for a couple of motorcycle clubs. He's a kid. This way, he can get a fresh—"

"Okay. Hold on. Hold the fuck on. He's *not* a kid, Charlie. He's a grown man. He goes with you because he feels guilty about pissing you off, but sooner or later you're going to realize you can't lead him around on a leash for the rest of his life."

"I'm not leading him on a leash. He agrees with me."

"He agrees because he doesn't want *you* to get hurt. He feels bad because he cares about you and didn't want you to get wrapped up in this. That's why he'd leave. But what you two don't understand is that moving away ain't going to fix anything."

She was quiet for a moment. "What do you mean?"

"I mean what I say. You think putting distance between Joel and the Fury will keep him safe? That's bullshit, Charlie. He knows too much about the club. They won't care what borders they have to cross. They'll find him."

She let out an uneven breath. "Is that true?"

"Yeah."

"How . . . is that how the Cobras operate, too?"

I shrugged. "We don't take betrayal lightly, but we're not like the Fury. They won't show a kid mercy just because he's a kid. I've seen it before with their prospects. In their eyes, the only way out of the club is death."

She gasped, and her hand flew to her mouth. She didn't say anything for a long time, and then I heard a quiet sob and realized she was crying.

"Hey," I said to her.

She continued to cry.

"Hey," I reached for her arm and drew her close, wrapping her up in a hug.

She sniffled. "Oh, God. It seems like there's no way out! It's hopeless," she wailed against my chest.

"No, it ain't."

"What do I do, then, Hart? Tell me what to do," she begged.

"What I've been telling you," I said, smoothing down her hair.

She looked up at me, and I could just make out her wide eyes in the darkness. "But how do you know that'll make things okay? If he goes with the Cobras, it'll just make them angrier."

"Because one of my brothers, Zain, was once a prospect for the Fury, and he lives every day with an X on his back. But the difference is, we're always protecting him, and they know if they fuck with him, they'll have to deal with our wrath. So they don't."

Her voice was small. "Can you do that for Jojo?"

"Yeah. That's the plan. That's how we'd get him out."

She pulled away and wiped at her eyes. "And the Cobras will do that for him?"

I nodded. "Yeah. The president of the Fury was fond of beating up on his wife and daughter. We took out Slade, and now we have his family in hiding. We take care of them. We could sure as hell do the same for you."

She let out a hard breath. "Both of us?"

"Yeah." She had crossed her arms in front of her, hugging herself, so I took hold of her forearm and pulled her closer. "Listen to me. This isn't just for Joel. I'd feel better if I was keeping an eye on you."

"Because they'll be after me, too." It wasn't a question.

"Yeah. They know about you. So they will be. But I'll keep you safe. If you trust me, Charlie, I'll keep you safe."

She nodded and lowered her head. "Thanks, Hart."

I wrapped my arm around her and she lifted her chin to me, begging to be kissed. My mouth descended on hers, and I tasted her. Tasted and kissed and plundered her mouth with my tongue for as long as I could stand it. She felt so right and perfect in my arms, I couldn't think of leaving. But I needed to get back to Nix.

When I broke the kiss, I didn't have to ask. She lifted my t-shirt up and started to kiss her way down my chest as I pulled it the rest of the way off. Her hands went to my belt buckle, and she tore my pants open, letting out hot little noises to tell me just how excited she was to get to me.

"You thirsty for something?" I asked her, taking hold of her ponytail to keep it out of the way.

She didn't answer. She was focused on one thing. I lifted my ass up to pull my pants down as she finished unzipping them and went for my cock, no hesitancy at all. She pulled it out, her tongue still hot on my abdomen, and started to palm my cock, making it harder.

Then she put her tongue on the tip. I leaned back onto my elbows and my head fell to the sky. She felt so damn good. I was glad it was dark because I was so damn horny for her, I couldn't fucking see straight.

When she licked down my shaft, my elbows buckled, and I nearly fell back on the table. I wanted, needed more of her, on me. She set to her work, taking the head into her mouth, and though I couldn't see more than her shadow, I knew her eyes were focused on me.

I groaned. "Fuck . . . that's good."

Her hot mouth slid up and down on my prick, her tongue going in circles, while she kept one slick finger and thumb wrapped around the base. It felt almost unbearably incredible, like a dream I'd soon wake up from. Grabbing her ponytail tight, I milked it, holding her there with her lips around my base for a couple of seconds before letting her resume her rhythm. She started going up and down, faster and faster on me, so I lifted up off the table and fucked her face.

Any more, and she was going to make me come. "Wait, Charlie . . . fuck. Wait," I said, nudging her away.

"Was that okay?"

"Fuck yes. But I want to be inside you."

She straightened and reached for the buttons of her shorts. "Do you have a condom?"

I'd been sure to restock after the last time. I reached for my wallet, pulled it out, and waved it in front of her as she shimmied out of her shorts. She laid them down on the bench and stood there, a little unsure as I ripped the condom package open and rolled it on.

I motioned her forward. "I'm going to get splinters, aren't I?" she said.

"Yeah. I've probably already got a few in my ass," I said. "But it'll be worth it. Get up here."

She took a step closer. I reached down and lifted her up, so she was straddling my lap. She knelt on the table on either side of me, her arms wrapped around my shoulder, her breath mingling with mine. She grabbed my cock underneath her and aimed it at her entrance.

Eye to eye, she slowly lowered herself down onto me. I let my hands fall down to her ass, grabbing the cheeks thinking how fucking perfect she fit me.

She started to grind on me, slowly, not up and down, but back and forth, rubbing herself on me and letting out little moans of pleasure. Slow, so agonizingly slow. She let out a sexy little whimper and her mouth dropped to my ear. "This okay?"

Like she had to ask? She was using me to get off. I felt her trembling, getting close. It fed my own lust, drawing me even closer. "Fuck yes. Keep going."

I reached up under her tank top and cupped her tits. They were perfect. Just two handfuls, the nipples already hard for me. "You feel so good," she whispered to me, her nose bumping against my ear. I dug my teeth into her shoulder. Her skin was so fucking sweet.

I wasn't going to last.

"Take it easy," I murmured, more for myself than for her, as she'd been moving more and more furiously, and I wanted to enjoy the ride a little longer.

She didn't listen. Lost in whatever trance she was in, she kept going, moving on me in a wild rhythm, feeling so fucking good. Her insides were so wet, so slick, so fucking heavenly, I couldn't remember a time when I'd felt this good. I growled as I thrust myself upward, gripping her hips and pulling her up, then jamming her back down onto me as I went off.

She shuddered, let out a little scream, and exploded a second later, falling, limp and boneless, on my chest. I let her spread herself out on me, with my cock inside her, just feeling the bones of her spine in the quiet of the night.

HART

As I held her, feeling her heartbeat against mine, I decided I'd destroy every single one of the Fury with my bare hands before I'd let them ever harm this sexy lady.

EVIE MONROE

Chapter Twenty

Charlotte

I left the Green Grove Park floating on air.

Even know the Fury might have eyes on us, Hart didn't let me walk home alone in the dark. Despite the few minutes' walk, he insisted on following behind me at a safe distance.

I stepped lightly, almost joyfully out of the park, feeling something inside me I'd never known before. And my cunt still throbbed like it had never throbbed before. Like I still had his fat cock in there, filling me up. Making me come. I shivered, and not from the chilly air. My heart felt like it had grown wings, the way it fluttered in my chest. I couldn't help looking over my shoulder at Hart and smiling like a goofy cartoon character.

When we got to the sidewalk outside my apartment complex, he revved his bike and tore off, giving me a little bit of a wave.

God, he was such a sexy beast. It made me warm inside, thinking of what we'd done.

When I reached our parking spaces in the lot, I saw Jojo's bike parked next to mine. I checked my phone. Eleven-fifteen. And he was probably wondering where the hell I was.

I climbed the stairs to the apartment, and sure enough, the light glowed from inside. When I put my key in the door, I heard the dogs barking, and expected I'd come in to find that Jojo had gone off to his room. But to my surprise, I found splayed out on the living room sofa, a half-empty bag of Doritos on his lap, watching television.

"Hey," I said.

"Hey," he said back, turning a glazed eye toward me. "You weren't at work. I thought they might have called you in."

"No. Wishful thinking. They cut my hours anymore, I don't know what I'll do."

He sat up. "So where were you?" He squinted at me. "And why are you smiling like that?"

I quickly ripped the smile off my face. "I just . . . went for a walk."

"Riiight." I could tell he didn't believe me for one second, but at least he didn't say what I knew was on his mind.

Instead, he said, "I just think that if you're going to get on me about where I am, it should work both ways."

I considered that for a quick minute. "Yeah. I guess. You're right. I didn't realize I'd be this late."

He leaned back and put his hands behind his head. "You're grounded."

I ripped a pillow from the sofa and tossed it at his head. He grabbed it and threw it back. The animals had a field day with us. Apparently deciding it was playtime, they all started to yelp.

Thinking of what Hart had said, I got up from the floor where Ernie had bounded on top of me and claimed the other end of the couch. "Am I really that big of a pain in the ass?"

He rubbed his jaw. "Let me think. *Yes.*"

That wounded me. After everything I'd done, I'd hoped he'd eventually come to be thankful for all of it. "Really?"

He cocked his head at me. "Really."

I bit my lip and took my punishment. "Okay, okay. I guess I deserve that. I know I've always been a little overprotective of you."

He groaned at the animals as they understood his trials and tribulations with his big sister. "A little?"

I went to smack him again, but this time he held up a pillow, so I wound up hitting that again. "All right. A lot. But I had my reasons. Foster care wasn't rainbows and sunshine. You know that. I wanted to protect you from that and the crappy foster parents we had. I wanted you to do great things. But I guess I failed you. I probably pushed you too hard."

He shook his head. "You didn't fail me. I was a rebel child." He chuckled a little, like he was trying on that label for size.

"Yeah. Because I kept pushing you to do good things. You rebelled."

"Maybe. But you were right. I realize that now. I was an ass. I probably should've listened to you."

I raised an eyebrow. "Really? Ya think?"

"Yeah, even the motorcycle clubs. I thought it'd be cool to be a badass and ride around on a big ass hog and have everyone quake in their boots when I rode into town like some big shit cowboy." He scoffed and added, "But I didn't want this bullshit. I didn't realize this would happen. I didn't know it would be a matter of life and death."

Tears came to my eyes, and my heart broke for him. He looked every bit the scared little kid, abandoned by his parents, beaten by his foster dad, and let down by every person who was supposed to look out for him. "Were you with the Fury, just now?"

He hung his head. "Yeah. They're bad dudes, Char. I thought it could get better once I wasn't a prospect and became a full member. But now I don't think it will. Scar—"

"Scar? Is he a Fury guy?"

"Yeah. He's . . . when I was there today, he told me they're testing me. And I have to do everything exactly as they say, or it's the end of the line for me."

I gasped. "What does that mean?"

Elbows on his knees, he pulled at his hair. "I don't know. He just said that if I didn't come the second I was called, they'd fuck me up and make it so I couldn't walk again, or worse. That's what they say to their *members*. They're supposed to be like a brotherhood, but they aren't. I'd hate to be their enemy."

"You know Hart said the Cobras would protect us."

"Yeah. I think Hart's a good man." He swallowed. "But I don't know how he'd feel if I told him . . . if I said . . ."

I leaned forward. "If you said what, Jojo?"

He let out a long breath and wiped his eyes, though I didn't see any tears there. "I'm done, Char. I want to tell them I'm done. All of them. I don't want any part of this. I don't want to join any club."

"Oh." It sucked to see him come to reason now, when it felt like it was too late. There had to be some way out. "Hart would understand."

"You really think so?"

I thought of Hart, and what he'd said to me. Now I believed that he truly cared about my little brother. Not just as a buddy, either—he probably thought of Jojo as the little brother he never had. I got the feeling that whatever Jojo wanted, he'd go along with it, as long as it would keep him safe.

"Yeah. I do. And I don't think he'd turn his back on us if you said you didn't want to join the Cobras, either. He'd help us. He says he can hide us away— they've hidden other people the Fury are after. The Cobras have kept them safe."

He gave me a doubtful look. "All right. Then that's what I want to do."

I sat down next to him, throwing my arm around him like I used to when he was younger. "We could move, too. Maybe not right away, because it's too dangerous. But in a few months, when the Fury stops looking for us."

I could tell he doubted it. "I know, I don't have any money. But I have a couple hundred saved up for emergencies. Once we know they're not looking for us anymore, we can just head out in my car and not stop until the gas runs out."

His face got all cloudy with worry and he protested my idea. "The Fury would probably find us. That's what Hart said."

"Not if we lay low for a little while under their protection first," I said brightly, squeezing him to me. "Remember when you and I were with the Mosely's?"

He looked at his knees and shrugged.

Of course he did. The Mosely's seemed too good to be true. They were religious people who lived in a mansion overlooking the bay. Mrs. Mosely was a fragile but sophisticated looking woman who worked as a lawyer, and Mr. Mosely, a handsome, geeky, mechanical engineer, had thick blond hair, and glasses and a smile as wide as the ocean. They had wealth and everything that came with it—except, they said, the blessing of children. They wanted to adopt as many children as possible. The day they drove us home, they talked about how they had a passion for travel and liked to go places almost every weekend. They asked if we'd mind that.

Mind that? We'd told them we'd love it, since we'd never been anywhere before, not even across state lines.

That first night, I remember looking at Jojo in awe. He had his own big bedroom, filled with model airplanes, Legos and Star Wars figures. Everything a kid his age would want. I was young and naïve, only fifteen, then.

It was maybe two months later that I woke up in that big, four-poster bed, and found Mr. Mosely naked next to me, with his hand in my panties. When I asked him what he was doing, he covered my mouth with his hand, climbed on top of me, and raped me.

I did all I could these days, not to think of that. How Mr. Mosely raped me every day for a month until I grew the balls and threatened to tell his wife. The next day, we were back in the foster system again. Jojo never understood it; thought he did something wrong, and I never told him.

But we had been on several day trips, before things turned bad. And that was what I wanted Jojo to concentrate on.

He nodded. "Barely. I was what . . . eight? Nine?"

"Yes. But you have to remember Santa Cruz. Right? The pier? I never saw you smile as much as you did that day. On that ride. You know, the one that goes all around?"

He laughed a little. "Yeah. You told me you were going to puke."

"Well, yeah. It was awful! The human body isn't meant to fall in little box like that."

"Maybe. But it was fun."

"Yeah. And I remember what you said to us all as we drove home. That when you were old enough you were going to live on that pier. You were going to live so that the first thing you could see every morning when you came out of your bedroom was the sand, and the Pacific, and the sea, and that pier."

Now, he was grinning. "Well. Yeah. I guess. I was stupid."

"No, that's not stupid! Let's do it! Even if we have to live in our car."

"With the animals?"

"I'll give them to Barb to watch over for us, just until we get settled. We can do it. You know we can. And Santa Cruz is big enough that we can probably get lost there and no one would find us."

He drummed his hands on his thighs, thinking. "Well . . . what about you and Hart?"

It would be hard, leaving Hart. He was the first guy I'd known who made me feel like there was such a thing as love. But I had to prioritize. "You know you come first. Always."

I hugged him close and put a big, wet, sloppy kiss on the unshaven whiskers of whatever beard he was trying to grow. He wiped at it and made a grossed-out face. "All right. All right. Then it's a go. Let's do it."

"Yeah? Are you really sure, Jojo?"

He nodded. "Yeah. Let's blow this joint."

I reached over to hug him, ruffling his hair like I used to when he was little. He groaned and protested, but I could tell he was happy, too.

When I sat up and I saw the mess of my apartment, the shit became real. I had to make lists, make a plan. Figure out everything I'd need to do before we went into hiding. I'd have to give notice at work. Ask Barb if she could watch the animals. Sell all the furniture. Hell on wheels, actually, for the next couple months. But so easy, really, I thought, compared to the horror waiting for us if we didn't go.

I felt like I could breathe easier now. Even Jojo, smiling for the first time in days, seemed as if a big weight had lifted off of him.

This would be great. It was the right decision. The only decision.

Hart would get over it. Me? I didn't think I'd ever forget him. Already he'd etched a place inside me no other man ever had. But I'd have to move on. For Jojo.

As I started to get up, Jojo's phone buzzed in his pocket. I checked the time on my phone. Who the hell was calling him after eleven thirty?

When he checked his screen and his face turned pale with dread, I knew. "Who is it?" I asked as he stared at the display. "That Scar character?"

He nodded.

"Don't answer!" I warned him. "You don't have to answer."

"I do. If I don't, they'll come after us," he said, swallowing so hard, his Adam's apple bobbed in his throat. He lifted the phone to his ear as I cringed. "Yeah?"

His voice sounded tough, but his other hand was shaking in his lap. I tried to grab it but he tensed and got up to pace as listened to a voice so loud, I could hear it roaring through the phone, though I couldn't make out the individual words.

"Yeah," he said after a minute. "I'll be there."

My stomach dropped down to my feet. *Fuck.*

He ended the call and threw his phone down on the coffee table as if it were crawling with bugs. "Fuck," he muttered, staring at the phone with contempt. He echoed my thoughts.

"They want you to meet them?" I asked.

He threw up his hands, his version of a disgusted *yes*.

"But you were just with them."

"They're testing me. To see how high I'll jump and how far."

"And so you have to go," I said. I didn't see any way out of it. Until we left town, he needed to do exactly what they said.

He looked up at me with pleading eyes, every bit that little boy who used to beg to go with me whenever the system would separate us into different foster homes. I still had to be the strong one, so I held back the tears.

"You'll be all right. Okay, Jojo?" This time he didn't object to the nickname. "Just do what they say, and in another week, another couple of days, you won't have to answer to them anymore. Trust me, Jojo. I promise you; it'll be okay."

I'd never lied to him before. When he'd go to another foster family who didn't want siblings, I always told him I'd come back to get him. And I fulfilled that promise. I was determined to deliver on this one, too. He must have been thinking that, too, because in the next few seconds, he drew in a breath and his face transformed. He stuck out his chin. "Yeah. All right."

He got up, pocketed his phone, and said, "I'll see you in a while, Char."

"Text me if you need me, okay?"

He gave me a brave thumbs up. Then he opened the door and stepped out into the night.

Chapter Twenty-One

Hart

I noticed Jojo's bike parked outside the apartment complex as I left Charlie there. Good. The kid was home. All was well.

But for how long?

I pulled off at a gas station to fill up, and texted Cullen: *Need to talk.*

When I replaced the gas nozzle, I checked my phone, and he'd already responded. *Come over. I'm home.*

I jumped on my bike and headed toward the ocean, where Cullen lived in his multi-million dollar mansion. I pulled into his long driveway, climbed the stairs, and rang the doorbell. A moment later, Grace answered, giving me the stink-eye through a mess of blonde hair.

"Sorry. Were you sleeping?" I asked her.

"No, but Ella is." She paused to listen for a moment. I heard the faint sound of a baby crying.

"Or *was,*" she said arching her neck. "Didn't Cullen tell you not to ring the doorbell?"

I shook my head as she pushed the door open, let me inside, then rolled her eyes.

Before she jogged up the sweeping foyer staircase, she said, "Figures. Sorry I can't be more hospitable, Hart, but I'm surviving on three hours of sleep a night. Ella might be an alien. I swear, she sleeps less than an hour a day."

"That sucks. You should get Cullen to do some of the heavy lifting."

"He does. But Ella drives us both insane." She reached the top of the landing and motioned down the hall. "He's in the theater."

I thanked her and headed down the massive marbled foyer to a narrower hallway decorated with electric guitars that Cullen's father, a famous rock guitarist, had played. Just this tiny section of the house was priceless. Cullen lived a bit of a charmed life in this rock-star home of his.

I saw the back of Cullen's head in the middle of the theater when I came to the open double doors, his feet up on the seat back in front of him. I couldn't place the movie on the screen that had his rapt attention. Some gangster flick, like one of the *Godfathers*.

"Hey," I said, climbing down the stairs and slipping into the row next to him. He was chewing noisily on what smelled like chewing tobacco.

He grabbed a remote and shut the movie off. "What's up?" he said, checking his phone. "It's late, dude. Didn't expect company. You want a . . ."

He looked around and threw up his hands.

"Fuck. I just finished the last beer. Sorry I don't have anything to offer you." He pulled out a packet of Nicotine gum. "You probably don't want this shit. I promised Grace I'd quit smoking for Ella. But I swear this is a fate worse than death."

I shook my head. I had more pressing things on my mind than filling my stomach. "I'm good."

"Everything okay?"

"You know, I have no idea. I've been thinking about the kid."

"The kid," he repeated, his eyes narrowing. "You mean Joel? Don't tell me he's turning on us."

"No. The opposite. He's loyal to us."

"That sounds good. So what's the problem?"

"What do you think is the problem? The Fury. They'll fuck him up if he turns on them."

Cullen punched out another piece of gum and stuck it in his mouth, crunching on it. "You think he wants to be one of us?"

"Yeah. That's what he said."

"You really think he's Cobras material?"

I wasn't sure about that. I thought that maybe he could be, if he didn't have Charlie helicoptering over him. But the thing was, having Charlie looking out for him wasn't a bad thing. She cared. Which meant he had a lot more than most of us Cobras had. A lot of us got into the club because we had no one else to count on.

I sure as hell did.

I rubbed the back of my neck and said, "That, I don't know. But I know he wants out of the Fury, and we're going to need to protect him and his sister from them once he makes that move."

"That's for sure. That, we can do. But . . . what about this sister of his?"

"Charlie. She's older. They've been on their own for a long time, so she's been looking out for him since they were kids. She's cool."

He raised an eyebrow. "So cool that you're fucking her?"

I shrugged. "I guess you could say we've been seeing each other."

"All right, all right," he said with a knowing laugh. "As long as your head's in the game, it's not a problem.

I just don't want this kid fucking us over because you've been blinded by pussy."

"No. It's not like that. I can tell the kid doesn't want any part of the Fury. The closer he got, the more he wanted to get away. And when I asked him about it, he told me he wanted out, and wants in with us."

"All right. All right." He rubbed his jaw, thinking. "Probably can't make that happen right away. It's too dangerous."

"Yeah. I propose we have the two of them lay low for now, and when the Fury move on, then he can join us. Kind of like what Zain did."

Cullen nodded. "Well, if the Fury's as much of a shit show as your boy seems to think, we shouldn't have much trouble taking them out and making it safe for your two friends to show their faces again."

"Sounds good."

"Then we'll have church tomorrow and put it to a vote what we want to do with him and see how soon we can make it happen. This girl of yours . . ."

"Charlie."

"Yeah. Charlie. Is she good with going into hiding under our protection for a little while? She's not going to put up a fight?"

"No. She knows what she's up against."

"Good. All right. I'll text everyone about church tomorrow."

He stood up, and I shook his hand. "Thanks, man."

As I was heading out, Grace came down the stairs with a sleeping Ella on her shoulder. "Have a good night," she whispered to me. I wished her one as well, and she closed the door behind me.

On my way back to my bike my phone started to buzz. "That's strange," I muttered. Why was Joel calling this late? From what I'd seen in the parking lot, he should have been at home with Charlie. "Hey," I said when I answered. "Everything okay?"

"Not really. The Fury just called me in," he said.

I realized I hadn't been looking too closely at his messages lately. In fact, I hadn't looked at his phone once all day. The result of his hot, fucking sister. If Cullen had known, he'd probably have reamed my ass, knowing I was supposed to be the one keeping tabs on him. I trusted Joel, but I'd been fucked by people I trusted before.

I'd have to do better.

What the fuck were the Fury motherfuckers doing to this kid? They'd just had him on a string, earlier in the day. They were definitely mind-fucking him, the assholes. It was a wonder anyone wanted to wear their patch.

"All right. Just go with the flow, man. Act natural, and nothing bad will happen, okay?"

It was more than I could do. I didn't think I could have put myself in a room with those dickwads, knowing what total fuckheads they were, and not want to punch every last one of them in the throat.

"Yeah," he said, but his voice sounded weak, like his resolve was crumbling. "I was wondering . . . my sister was freaking out when I left her. Could you go and . . .?"

"Sure," I said. I'd decided to go over there, anyway, the moment he said the Fury had called him in again. "Don't worry about her. Leave her to me."

"Thanks. I'm just worried about her being home. Alone."

"Tell you what, I'll pick her up and bring her back to my place. No one will think to fuck with her there. All right?"

"Yeah. Okay. That's good. Thanks, Hart."

"No problem. Just text me when you can. And be careful."

I ended the call and revved my bike, gunning it toward Charlie's apartment. It was nearly midnight. I thought she might be asleep, but when I got there, I spotted a light in the window. When I climbed the stairs, someone's shadow move behind the blinds.

I used my manners and knocked softly on the door so I wouldn't disturb the neighbors.

The sound of barking erupted from inside.

She answered a split second later. "You ought to be careful who you open the door for," I said jokingly. Or maybe not.

She fisted one hand on her hip and pointed at the peephole with the other. "Why are you here?"

I stepped back, in part from the shot of her cold greeting and in part to take her in. Since our crazy hot minute in the park, she had changed into boxers and a camisole so sheer I could see her nipples through the fabric. A big, shapeless cardigan and big socks. She'd piled her hair on her head casual like so strands fell around her neck, and she rocked ridiculous horn-rimmed glasses I'd never seen before, kind of like Harry Potter. She looked like a nerd. A fucking hot wet dream of a nerd.

"You're coming with me."

She raised an eyebrow. "Oh? Why?"

"Because Joel called me and told me where he was headed and asked me to take care of you."

She smirked. "You think I need you to take care of me?"

I smirked back. "I think you'd *rather* I take care of you, than you do it alone."

She motioned me inside. "Come in before the animals get out."

She closed the door behind me. The animals started to get riled, attacking my ankles for a chance to get petted. I leaned down and let them smell my hands, then offered a few strokes.

"I knew you didn't hate animals," she said with a note of triumph in her voice.

I straightened, ignoring the fluffy little thing leaning into me, wanting more of my attention. "Hate's a strong word. But I don't like them, either."

She closed the door and crossed her arms over her chest. "Where are we going?"

"My place."

"On your death trap?"

I nodded. "You can have my helmet. It's only a short drive."

The sly, teasing smirk disappeared and a wrinkle appeared on her forehead. "But what about Jojo? What if he comes back?"

"I told him to text me and let me know what's up."

She looked around. "Let me change and get some things first."

I took her hand. "You're fine like that. I like the getup."

She looked down at herself, and her glasses slipped from the bridge of her nose. Going to push them back up, she realized she was wearing them and quickly yanked them off.

"I didn't know you wore glasses."

"Reading glasses," she said, motioning to the massive open book tented on the coffee table. *The*

Stand by Stephen King. "I couldn't sleep. I never can when Jojo's out."

I lifted the book. "You ever read this before?"

She shook her head.

"It's one of his best," I told her, setting it down.

"I didn't realize you were a reader."

I shrugged. "I'm more into non-fiction."

She took the book from my hands and said, "One minute. Let me just pack some things for tomorrow, okay?"

She put the book back on the table and I waved her goodbye. As she headed for her bedroom, I walked around the living room with a parade of animals at my feet, really getting a chance to take in my surroundings, the shabby furniture, mostly second-hand thrift store shit. Like the coffee table made out of a slab of wood, standing on two milk crates.

But out of everything in the cramped living room, the photographs grabbed my attention more than anything else. She had dozens of them on the walls, all from different times of her life, but the one similarity? They all contained just her and Joel. Never anyone else. Even the pictures of her as a young girl, probably no more than twelve or thirteen years old. Like she was making a statement: the two of them against the world.

She'd said as much. She hadn't given me details about herself, but she'd said that Joel hadn't had the easiest life, and she'd been watching over him since she was young.

A second later, as I was looking at a picture of the two of them in front of the roller coaster in Santa Cruz, I saw her face reflected in the glass, behind me. "That was a long time ago," she said softly.

"You look happy."

She gnawed on her lip. "I was. The only problem is that happiness doesn't last."

"It's not something that just happens," I said, surprising myself at the words of wisdom coming out of my mouth. "It's something you make. Something you choose."

She let me know her opinion with the scoffing sound that flew out of her mouth. "Yeah. Right. Tell it to that girl right there. Last real smile I remember. Fifteen years old and about to be raped by her foster father every night for a month."

I just stared at her. Well, now the mystery surrounding my sweet, hot Charlie had been blown wide open. "Jesus," I breathed.

As if she hadn't said anything, she leaned down and picked up one of her mutts, stroking it on its fuzzy black head. "Bye Bert. Bye Ernie. Opie. Mags."

She blew them all kisses, slung a backpack over her shoulder, and strode to the door.

I hadn't moved.

She looked back expectantly at me; her face was devoid of any emotion. "Don't tell Jojo. He doesn't know."

So she was keeping things from her brother, while trying to raise him right. "What else doesn't he know?"

She didn't answer. She just stared at me, like, *Can we go now?*

I followed her out to my bike, slipped the helmet on her, and adjusted it so it didn't fall over her eyes. The strap was loose, but it'd do for the ride. I didn't live more than a mile away. "Climb on," I said, still not sure what to say about her revelation. "And just hold onto me tight."

She did, wrapping her arms tightly around my waist as I gunned the motor and we took off toward my place. I felt her thighs squeezing me, her tits pressed up against my back, her face buried in my shoulder blades. "You okay?" I asked over my shoulder as we pulled up to a red light.

"Yes," came the soft reply.

"You can relax a little, baby. Any tighter and I won't be able to breathe."

"Oh. Sorry." She loosened her grip on me and we made it the rest of the way without any more of her death grips.

"Here we are," I said when I pulled into a parking space.

She looked up. I think she may have had her eyes closed. "Oh, thank God. That was . . . frightening beyond all belief."

I couldn't help laughing. I got the feeling she'd been through some very heavy shit, if that story about her foster family and the way she protected her brother had been any indication. For her to be scared on a bike? She was one funny girl.

When I opened the door to my apartment, she went inside and her eyes immediately fell on the robotic arm on the coffee table. I hadn't done any work on it in a week.

"Nice conversation piece," she observed, walking to my desk where I kept all of my computers and parts. She didn't say anything, but then she walked to the bookcase and started reading some of the titles there. "Oh, my God."

I had my hands in the pockets of my jeans, just watching her. "What?"

"You're a nerd?"

I grinned and hitched a shoulder.

She turned and looked at me, wide-eyed. "Oh, my God, Hart. Do you actually like to tinker and build computers and code and shit?"

I grinned over the flush of pleasure at her interest in what I did. "What can I say? You discovered my secret."

She shook her head, clearly amused, then made the motion of zipping her lips and throwing away the key. "I won't tell a soul. Would probably damage your rep with the ladies, you know?"

"Yeah? Well, there's only one lady whose opinion I care about right now."

"Oh?" She slipped her cardigan off and threw it on the sofa. Then she slowly came toward me, looking so hot and sexy with her nipples pressing right through her camisole that I was hard by the time she got close.

She wrapped her arms around me, lacing them around my neck. I inhaled the scent of apples as she stood on her tiptoes and whispered in my ear, "You want to know my opinion?"

I looked hungrily into her eyes and waited for the answer.

"My opinion is that you should take me to your bedroom. Right now."

I wasted no time in scooping her up and carrying her down the hall.

EVIE MONROE

Chapter Twenty-Two

Charlotte

Hart gently set me down on his bed and peeled off his t-shirt. I sat up on my elbows while he stared at me.

"What? Don't tell me you're at a loss for what to do?" I teased him.

He moved forward, spanning the distance in a heartbeat. At first I thought he was going to crush his mouth onto mine and fuck me hard and fast, the way he'd done before. But when he was at the edge of the bed, he slowly lifted one of my legs and peeled off my big, woolen sock. Eyes never leaving mine, he teased my ankle with a kiss.

Then, he slowly peeled off the other sock, his breath coming hard and raspy.

He tossed them to the side and kissed my other ankle. Kissed my toes. Licked his way down the arch of my foot while his hand trailed down my calves, to my thigh.

"Anyone every tell you that you have phenomenal . . ."

He paused then, his tongue flicking its way up my leg. "Phenomenal . . . what?" I asked.

"Everything," he said, reaching down and grabbing the hem of my boxer shorts. He pulled them off, and because I wasn't wearing any panties, he left me bare. He gazed at me as if he'd never seen a naked woman before. "All of you. It's perfect."

I smiled and fell back off my elbows, basking in the compliment. I'd had many men call me things. *Whore. Worthless. Trash.* But this was the first time anyone had called me *perfect.*

I couldn't say I believed it. Not yet. Still, the way he looked at me, so intensely, he could've had me believing anything.

My whole body tingled as he crouched at the side of the bed, held me by my ankles and dragged me forward. "Is this okay?"

"Oh yes," I purred.

"Tell me what you want. Always tell me."

My voice came out as a croak. "You. Anything you want to do."

He pressed a finger against my lips. "No, sweetheart. I want to do what *you* want me to do. What makes you feel good."

I almost laughed. Everything he did made me feel good.

But then I realized that he was doing this because of my confession to him. Maybe I shouldn't have told him. It was a leap of faith, even just to make that admission. I'd never told anyone before, because there were some men out there—and I'd met them—who wouldn't have cared. Who would've treated me like the whore they all said I was.

Not Hart. He crouched between my legs; his jeans tented with his hard cock. Waiting for me to tell him how to please me.

I fell a little bit in love with him at that moment.

"Um. Kiss me."

He lifted his mouth to mine and brushed his lips against them, just a soft, dry kiss, but it made my nipples pucker and my body quiver with need. When he pulled away, his eyes dropped down to my bare pussy, and he planted his hands, one on each thigh.

"Touch me."

"Sure." He dipped his tongue into my mouth, and as he did, he gently touched my clit, rubbing in soft, slow circles. His other hand cupped my face, thumb rubbing my throat, up to my chin. His mouth trailed to my earlobe, sucking on it, as his thumb swept across my lip, into my mouth. I tongued it eagerly, sucked it for all I was worth, losing all sense of myself.

Maybe he could see that I didn't believe him, because he buried his face in my neck. "You're so fucking beautiful," he breathed into my ear.

I didn't react. I guess I didn't know how.

Then he covered my throat with his big hand and tilted my face so that I had no choice but to look into his eyes. "You understand?"

I nodded dumbly. Because it didn't matter what he told me. He could've called me worthless, and I would've reacted just the same. I wanted him, no matter what. I was so completely his.

"Do you want my finger inside you?"

I nodded, helpless.

He slowly inched a finger inside and began to move it in and out. The way way he took his time, so sexy and sweet, letting me know he cared what I needed, I could barely breathe. "Yes. That's good."

"More?"

I nodded because I couldn't even speak.

He added a finger and started to thrust into me, fucking me with expert fingers. I shuddered, my hands gripping his hard shoulders, as he held me in place, only letting me move to rock my hips to his thrusts.

I wanted more. He pushed himself closer, spreading my legs impossibly wide, going faster. Faster. His other hand dragged from my throat to my breast, squeezing it, tweaking my nipple hard. I opened my mouth, panting ragged breaths like an animal in heat as he continued his assault. My body was so hungry, so starved, I wanted everything he could give me.

He set his forehead on mine and continued driving his fingers into me, palming my clit. He seemed to revel in the moans of pleasure he tore from my throat. Ripples of feeling shot across my body, spiraling out as he milked me closer and closer to the edge, rubbing and thrusting with a rhythm that made me shake.

I tensed and came so hard, I threw my body against his chest. I would've sunk right into the mattress if he hadn't been there to hold me still. He held his fingers inside me, as my pussy contracted and I gushed all over the bed. I moaned and cried like a puppy, staring at him in disbelief.

"What are you thinking?" he asked.

I debated for a moment whether to tell him, then decided I was bare naked on his bed—there was no reason to have any shame now. "You're the first man who has ever made me come."

"Yeah?" He kept his forehead pressed up against mine, breathing hard. "That's a goddamn shame."

"I'd honestly started thinking I didn't work that way. That something was wrong with me."

"Trust me, baby. There's nothing wrong with you." He lifted his forehead from mine. The look on his face was pure, badass male pride as he slid his sopping wet hand from my pussy, brought his fingers to his mouth, and sucked my juices. "You taste good."

I tried to sit up and look for my boxers, wherever they'd gone, using the sheet to cover myself. He tugged my hand away and slipped a hand between my damp thighs.

"Don't think I'm done with you, yet," he said, slipping a finger under my chin and lifting my mouth to his. He nibbled sexily at my lips, and I could taste myself on his tongue.

"What did you have in mind?" I asked.

"No. It's whatever *you* have in mind."

I sat up, grabbing him by the waistband of his jeans, and dragged him toward me. I climbed up to my knees on the bed, pressing my tits up against his body, and he groaned low in his throat. He reached for the fabric of my tank top, the only thing between us now, yanking it out of shape so that my breasts popped out of the armholes. "This is a good look for you."

I smiled. "Oh, yes, this is the new fashion trend. Women will be wearing it like this on the streets next spring."

"Fuck no. I want these tits all to myself," he said, dipping his head and licking lightly at a nipple. "They're too precious to let just anyone see."

I unbuckled his jeans, slipping the zipper down and sliding the jeans over the magnificent curve of his ass. His cock sprang free, hard and ready for me.

The moment I saw it, I couldn't help myself. I had a one-track mind. My mouth went wet and my pussy clenched. "Please. Just fuck me."

He let out a chuckle, and I could tell my request was one he wouldn't deny. He had one arm still wrapped around my waist, and he lifted me up, cradling my ass in his arms. I wrapped my legs around him, feeling that massive hard length of steel trapped between us.

Then he dragged his lips to mine, nipping at my lips with his teeth in a savage way before plunging his tongue into my mouth again.

I wrapped my arms around his neck, tighter, as his tip touched my entrance. His hands were so big, holding my ass firmly, cupping it, squeezing it. I tilted my pelvis forward, sucking in a breath in anticipation as he slowly lowered me onto his cock so that was sat facing each other.

When he'd found just the right spot, he rocked his hips forward in one sudden movement, meeting me halfway, tearing a raspy moan from my throat.

Every muscle in my body tensed. My head fell back and I inhaled. He held me up as he pushed deeper into me and then began a slow thrust. It was only moments before I felt myself tightening around him. The tight stretch made my orgasm retreat for a moment, but when his thumb began to rub my clit again, it came back with a vengeance and hit me like a freaking freight train. I heard myself scream as I clenched around his thick cock. I sank my nails into his shoulders as I pressed into him, coming and coming and coming.

But he wasn't finished. No, he was a man possessed.

He looked like an animal, his face rigid with raw concentration as he fucked me, slowly, steadily. "Come on, baby," he goaded me. I felt the fire building inside, starting low in my belly and screaming through me. "Come, Char. Come on."

I felt the fire building inside me again. He asked, and I did as I was told. The tension overwhelmed me, sensations bursting inside me one after the other. I had no need for breath as I fell against him, crushing my mouth to his. I kissed him hard, urgent, the world going dark and blurry around me. I hadn't meant to scream, but oh God, did I scream. He ripped his mouth free, grabbed my hips and stared into my eyes, pressing his forehead against mine.

"There you go, baby," he growled, lifting his hips off the blanket and thrusting deep inside me. "Come with me."

I met that thrust with an explosion of pleasure, my eyes rolling back to the sky, fireworks exploding behind my eyelids. He groaned and exploded inside me, gripping my hips and tensing around me.

My scream faded to a whimper, and just when I thought I was done, he rocked into me, stroking my swollen clit, prolonging my orgasm. I couldn't find the voice to scream anymore. I just let the smaller ripples lap over me, as my body fell into a pile of mush.

I collapsed against his chest, my body heaving. Resting my cheek on his collarbone as small aftershocks coursed through my body, I finally understood what true happiness felt like.

"Um. Wow," I said, shell-shocked. "That was . . . wow."

He slipped out of me and rolled onto his side, gazing at me. "Good?"

Beyond good. I did the bobble-head nod again, wishing I could think of an exact word to describe it. Heavenly, Amazing, Incredible . All seemed to miss the mark. I was sweaty and sticky with his come, and so, so satisfied, like I could have the best night of sleep I'd ever had.

He kissed the tip of my nose gently. "Good. Come here."

He pulled me to his hard chest, spooning me against his warm, solid muscles, with his cock nestled firmly against the crack of my ass. It felt like slipping into a space that was perfectly made for me. He draped a muscled arm around my waist, holding onto my hands.

"Okay?"

"Yes," I breathed.

I felt more than okay. For the first time ever, I felt completely safe.

"Hart," I whispered after a moment. "When I told you about . . . what I told you . . . before?"

"Um-hmm," he said, kissing my ear. "It's all right. You don't have to explain anything."

I exhaled. "I want to, though. I want to tell you everything." I chuckled a little. "I've never told anyone about it before. But you're the first person I can trust. I never had . . . anyone."

His breath was hot on my neck. "What about your parents?"

I sucked a deep breath. "My mom used to panhandle with us. Sitting right outside the supermarket, with a cardboard sign that said she couldn't feed us. She said our cute faces got us more money. Even if we were hungry, she'd only take money."

"Wow. Did you—"

"Hush. Let me talk, okay? Every time someone came offering us food or a place to stay, she'd tell them no. She knew exactly how much money was in that can at all times. The second she had enough for a bag of heroin, she'd hand it to my dad, he'd go off and score it, and then they'd shoot up right there in the parking lot. Then . . . right back to panhandling." I wiped a tear that threatened to fall.

"You're fucking with me."

"No, and what was so sad was I thought it was my fault. God, I was so young, maybe seven, when I heard her talking to some guy, trying to sell us for drug money. At the time, I remember being happy about it. I thought if someone bought us, they'd treat us better."

"Shit, Charlie."

"So we went to the gas station where the deal was supposed to happen. Jojo was just a baby. Maybe two? Three? And the police showed up. My parents jumped in our car and sped away. That was the last time we ever saw them. They were so fucked up at that point, they didn't even notice they'd left us behind."

"Damn, Charlie. I'm sorry. Sorry you had to go through that."

I took another breath and let it out. "Since then, we'd been in foster care. Bouncing around all over the place. Sometimes a foster family would take siblings, sometimes they wouldn't. We didn't have a choice. But I promised Jojo that the second I turned eighteen, I'd get out on my own, and I'd take care of him and raise him the right way. It wasn't easy. But I did it."

"You're damn right, you did. You're fucking hardcore. Anyone ever tell you that?"

I smiled. "No, been called a lot of things, but hardcore isn't one of them. I never wanted a thank you for just doing what it took to make sure my brother and I survived, and that was a good thing, because I never got one. I figure that one day, ten years from now, when Jojo is grown with a job and a family of his own, he might look back and say thank you. If he doesn't, no biggie. When you love someone as much as I love him, you're bound to put up with a lot of little injustices like that."

"You are a great lady, Charlotte."

"Thanks." I yawned and settled up against Hart's body, wishing I could stay there forever.

It was only as I was drifting off to sleep that I realized he came in me hard, and we hadn't used a condom.

Chapter Twenty-Three

Hart

I fell asleep, cradling Charlie in my arms, dragging in the apple scent of what must've been her shampoo, and I held her close against my chest.

What seemed like only seconds later, I heard a faint buzzing and realized it was my phone, vibrating on the nightstand.

I reached over to grab it and squinted in the green glow of my digital clock. It said three in the morning.

Kissing Charlie on her bare shoulder, I pulled my arm from hers and slid out of the bed, grabbed the phone, and looked at the display.

What did Joel want?

Moonlight slashed in through the blinds, illuminating a faint smile on Charlie's pretty face. I didn't want to wake her, so I quickly headed out of the bedroom and closed the door. As I padded down the hallway naked, I answered. "Hey, kid," I said, throwing myself down on the sofa. "You okay?"

"Hart?"

Shit. I could tell from that one word that things were most definitely not okay. He sounded like a wounded little kid. Like he'd been crying.

I sat up straight. "What's going on, Joel? Talk to me."

"I think I'm in trouble."

After Charlie had poured her little heart out to me, I'd gone to sleep last night knowing exactly what I had to do. At all costs, I'd protect Joel. He didn't just mean a lot to her. He was her whole life. From what she'd said, I'd learned she spent a lot of her time bearing the brunt of the world's shit, just so he wouldn't have to.

Protecting him like that might have been a mistake, because he didn't have the tools to deal with the situation he was in right now.

But the poor kid hadn't known what kind of hornet's nest he was stepping on. Neither did Charlie.

Unlike Joel, though, she had balls. Knowing her, she would've run down to the Hell's Fury clubhouse and demanded they leave him alone.

I couldn't let her do that. She'd get herself killed.

"What trouble?" I said, hoping that he'd just blown a tire on his way home. Something simple and fixable.

But then he said the thing that made me curse under my breath and punch the coffee table with my fist. All the little pieces of the arm I was tinkering with went flying in all directions. He said, "I think they know."

I took a deep breath and set my jaw. "You think who knows?"

"The Fury. I think they know I'm working with you guys." He voice cracked on the last word, and he let out a low groan. "What the fuck am I going to do?"

"All right. Calm down," I said, standing up and pacing. As I did, I stepped on a bolt with my bare foot, and clenched my teeth, kicking it out of the way. "Okay, start from the beginning. Why do you think that?"

"They have photos, Hart. Of you and me meeting somewhere. I don't know. They didn't even point them out to me." His words came out in a tumble. "They just fucking left them on the bar for me to find. I mean, they were grainy. But I'm pretty fucking sure it was obvious that it was you and me."

I covered the speaker with my hand and gritted my teeth. "Fuck!" I growled.

I took a minute to consider my options. Why would they not tell him about them, unless they were fucking with him? Unless they didn't realize it was him and me in the photos?

"Okay," I finally said to him, calming myself. "Are you absolutely sure, that it was obvious to them that they'd nailed you and me? Could they have thought it was someone else?"

"No. No, I'm pretty sure they know it was me. Because when I got there they were acting weird. And then they kept making me go over to the bar to get them drinks, so I would see them. I'm telling you, Hart, they know."

"All right, all right. Just play it cool. Where are you now?"

"I'm on my bike. I just pulled over onto the side of the road to call you. I don't know what to do." I could hear it in his voice, the panic rising, getting more and more frantic as we spoke. He was definitely *not* playing it cool. "Shit, man. Shit. What do I do?"

"Listen to me," I barked out, turning toward my bedroom door. It remained closed, which was good. I didn't want Charlie coming out so I'd have to deal with two hysterical people. Wherever he was, he was breathing hard and cursing under his breath. "Listen. Joel. Are you listening?"

He sniffled. "Yeah."

"Do you know if any of them followed you?"

"Uh. No. I don't think so. I mean. I don't see anyone. I don't . . ."

"All right. I want you to go to the Cobras clubhouse. Right now. Don't stop for anything. I'll text the guys and let them know you're on your way. Someone's usually there on the weekend. Knock twice on the door when you get there, and they'll let you in. You got it?"

"Uh. Okay. I guess."

I heard a noise down the hallway, toward my bedroom, which I chalked up to an open window and the curtains blowing in the night air. I'd have to get to the clubhouse right away. And I'd have to bring Charlie. She couldn't stay here alone; it wasn't safe.

"All right. I'll be there in ten minutes, Joel, and I'll bring your sister. Okay?"

"Yeah. Good. All right."

"Stay calm, kid."

I hung up and dragged a hand over my face. This wasn't fucking good. The kid couldn't start cracking. I could only imagine he hadn't kept it together at the

Fury meeting, either. He probably had his guilt written all over his face.

I quickly checked the tracker on his phone. He wasn't too far from the clubhouse—maybe a ten-minute ride away. Good. He was out of the belly of the beast, at least.

Poor kid. All he had to do was get to the Cobra clubhouse. That was it. After that, we'd keep him safe.

I sent a group text to the other officers: *URGENT: Hell's Fury knows about Joel. Heading to clubhouse now. Let him in and keep him there.*

A second later, I got a text back from Zain: *Shit. I'm here. I'll let him in.*

Moments after that, as I headed back to the bedroom, a text came in from Jet: *Heading there now. FUCK THE FURY.*

The rest of the guys sent texts as well, letting me know they had my back. I opened the door and saw Charlotte sitting up in bed, the sheets pulled up to her chest. "Is everything okay?"

I grabbed her backpack and handed it to her. "Nope. We've run into a little situation. Get dressed and I'll explain," I said, finding my jeans on the floor and stepping into them.

Her eyes widened with worry. I knew she was thinking of just one person. The only person who ever really existed in her life. Her brother, who meant more to her than anything else in this world.

Chapter Twenty-Four

Charlotte

A situation could've been anything. A lost sock. A clogged toilet. Anything.

But I knew it had to do with Jojo. And though Hart wasn't one to overreact, or even react strongly to very much, I knew it was something bad.

"What kind of situation?" I asked, holding the backpack on my lap and undoing the zipper.

He pulled his t-shirt on over his chest and ran his hands through his long hair before pulling it back into a ponytail. Then he sat down to put on his boots. He motioned with his chin to the bag. "Hurry up."

I grabbed a t-shirt and jeans out of the bag and started to fish around for my panties. I couldn't find them, and he was making me nervous, watching me as he tied his boots. "Is it about Jojo?"

"I'll tell you on the way," he muttered, grabbing his vest and putting it on.

Not finding panties, I decided I'd go commando. I'd put on my jeans and stood with my hands on my hips. "I'm not going anywhere until you tell me what this is about."

He reached for my shirt, opened it up, and brought it down over my head, so that only part of my face made it through the neck-hole. I didn't have a bra on, either, but at that point, I had other things to worry about. "Hart. You're making me nervous."

He didn't answer me. He stormed out of the room, pocketing his phone. I found flip-flops and scuffed my feet into them, raking my hands through my messy hair as I rushed to keep up with him. When he reached for the door, I threw myself against it and closed it.

"I'm not playing. Tell me, dammit, Hart."

He sighed. "All right. Fine. It looks like Hell's Fury knows that your brother's been meeting with us and helping us out."

I suddenly couldn't breathe. "Wait. I thought you said they wouldn't find out. That he'd be safe. You promised me."

"I know. I did. We were careful. But they found out anyway and now he could be in danger. So we've got to go. Now."

I felt like the floor had dropped out from under me. My knees weakened as I stared at him in sheer disbelief. "But you said—"

"I said we'd protect him. And that's what we're doing. Now, let's fucking go."

I covered my mouth with both hands. "If anything happens to him . . ."

"Nothing will. I'll make sure of that."

I didn't know what to believe. If I lost Jojo, I'd die. But I wasn't thinking straight. I'd just had the most amazing night of my life and convinced myself Hart was borderline immortal and could do anything he wanted. Now, I wasn't so sure.

I grabbed the door handle. "All right. Let's go."

Once outside, we ran into a pitch-black wall.

I jumped on Hart's bike without waiting for him to put the helmet on me. When he did, I said, "Hurry, hurry." All I could think about was Jojo in trouble. Jojo needing me. That he couldn't deal with this on his own. That Hart may have said he would protect us, but I was the one who'd always been responsible for protecting my brother.

To think, I'd been so scared while riding on Hart's bike, before. I kept looking at the pavement and worried we crash and I'd get splattered all over it. But when we sped off toward the clubhouse, I didn't even think about the death trap. All that mattered was my brother.

Hart drove down a long, deserted pier, toward the ocean. The dark sky looked so calm, just a thin line of blue separating it from an equally calm Pacific. I squeezed my arms around Hart's waist, trying to think positive thoughts.

When he pulled to a stop in front of a one-story warehouse, I saw a number of motorcycles, too many bikes to pick Jojo's out, but I hoped his was among them.

Hart slipped the helmet off of my head and said, "Come on."

I followed him and he rapped on the door. A second later, someone answered. It had to be a member of his club—a jacked guy with tattoos and a *fuck you* expression on his face. They fist-bumped and he let us in.

Hart said, "Jet, this is Charlotte, Joel's sister. Is he here yet?"

Jet gave me a surly look and shook his head. "Not yet."

And I totally lost it.

"He isn't?" I shouted, getting frantic. "Where is he?"

Jet closed the door and drew the blind closed again as Hart wheeled on me, placing his hands on my shoulders. "Hey. Listen to me. Everything's okay. He'll be here any minute now."

I reached for the doorknob. "Well, I want to go out and—"

He grabbed me and pulled me away from the door. "Charlie. It's not—"

"Let me go!" I snarled, yanking away from him

"*NO*," he barked, making me freeze in my tracks. He'd never raised his voice like that before, and it had the desired effect. He drew me away from the door. "It's not safe. You need to stay here. If anything, I'll go out and look for him, okay?"

His eyes burned intently on mine, making it impossible to disagree. At the same time, I realized we had an audience. My eyes trailed to his side to a long folding table, where five other guys sat smoking, each one bigger and more threatening than the next. Every eye in the place glared at me.

I gulped. "Okay."

He noticed me looking at them and said, "Come on. Take a load off for a minute and meet the guys."

Guys? These were more like monsters than guys. My worst nightmares. But I guessed I'd thought the same about Hart when I met him. I meekly followed him to the group.

"Guys, this is Charlotte. Charlotte, this is Nix, and Zain. And over there is Drake. Cullen. And you already met Jet."

I nodded and peeped out a scared little, "Hi."

The one I think Hart had called Cullen pulled out a chair next to him. "Hey, Char. Come and sit down. Can we get you anything to drink?"

I shook my head, and because they were still looking at me, I sat at the very edge of a seat.

Hart went to the fridge, grabbed a Coors, twisted the lid off, and handed it to me. "Just have it. Relax."

I took a tentative sip, my knees shaking.

Hart pulled out his phone and started scrolling through it. Whatever he saw, he didn't like, because he nodded at Cullen, who stood up. "All right. Let's go."

I jumped up too. "What? Where are you going?"

Hart avoided looking at me for the longest time, heading to the door with his head down. I grabbed him before he could get very far. "He's my brother. Are you going to tell me what's going on?"

He looked over at Cullen, and then held up his phone with an attitude of resignation. "I told you I was looking out for your brother. Even when I wasn't with him, I was still keeping tabs on him. I put a tracking device on his phone."

"You did?"

He nodded, a sheepish look on his face.

Of course he did. He was a closet computer nerd. No wonder he hadn't been too concerned when Jojo had gone off with the Fury before. But now, looking at Hart, I knew there was something else he was reluctant to tell me. I was getting good at reading Hart when he was trying to keep stuff from me. "And you can tell where he is? So where is he?"

"He was on his way here, when you and I left my apartment. He was only a few minutes away," Hart said, not meeting my eye. "Now he's downtown. Near the canning district."

"The canning district?" I repeated, trying to get it through my head. That was where heroin addicts went to score. It was just blocks and blocks of burned-out old factories and homeless people and thugs. There was no reason for a normal person to go there.

My heart thrummed in my chest. I brought my hands to my cheeks. "Oh, God."

Hart held out his hands. "Look, we don't know—"

"Yes we do! He'd never go there on his own! They have him! And if they know what he did, they'll kill him! I'm coming with you."

Hart shook his head adamantly. "You definitely are *not*. It's too dangerous."

"But I have to! He's my brother! What can I—"

He placed his hands solidly on my shoulders, holding me there, but even that didn't stop my body from trembling.

"Charlie," he said, low so the others wouldn't hear. "We'll take care of it. I'll bring him home."

Tears filled my eyes. He'd made promises before. "Will you?"

He put a finger under my chin, tilting my face up to his, and set a soft, dry kiss on my lips. "I'll do my best, sweetheart. Just promise me you'll stay here."

I nodded, and Hart and Cullen grabbed their helmets and swept out of the room without another look back.

They seemed so confident, like this was business as usual.

But I was pretty sure I was going to have a heart attack. And it only occurred to me as I heard their bikes roaring into the distance, that Hart was in just as much danger as Joel was. And I hadn't even given him a proper goodbye.

That was because he had made it seem like it wasn't a big deal. But what if it was the last time I ever saw him?

As I slumped down in the chair, my stomach turned as I realized with a sickening feeling that I couldn't bear to lose either of them.

EVIE MONROE

Chapter Twenty-Five

Hart

We left Charlotte at the clubhouse with Jet and Nix, and the rest of us headed out in search of Hell's Fury. Normally, we didn't know where they'd meet, since they kept their clubhouse a secret and kept changing locations. But because I had a GPS tracker on Joel's phone, I knew exactly where to find them.

The other men wanted to unleash a little hell on the Fury, but by the time I'd made it to my bike, a sick feeling had settled in my stomach. I never liked walking in on Fury turf. And now, they had one massive bargaining chip in their clutches.

Joel. I couldn't let them hurt him. I'd promised Charlie.

They were down in the shit section of town, the canning district, home to the burned-out old businesses. Not far from the old ribbon factory where Zain and I had gotten caught up. Ground Zero. There'd likely be bloodshed tonight, and no police to break things up when shit got bad.

Maybe she already knew, but I didn't want to tell Charlotte that. She worried enough as it was.

Hell, even I was fucking worried.

The night fell silent, as if it, too, held its breath, waiting for something bad to happen. Everything seemed to lead up to this big moment, a moment that would go down in the history of the two clubs. As we left the clubhouse, we all loaded our pieces.

"You think they're expecting us?" Drake asked as he threw a leg over his bike.

I shrugged. If they were, it made sense why I'd tracked the phone to Ground Zero. Even the police didn't like to go there. There, it could get as bloody as they wanted it to, and no one would arrive to break it up. Maybe that was what they were counting on. "Could be."

We all climbed on our bikes and revved them up, heading away from the pier. At this hour of the night, the streets were deserted. It'd been a long night.

And if anything happened to Joel, it'd only get longer.

As we rode, I took out my phone and tried to gauge the location via the GPS. Based on the map, it looked like he was still in the parking lot of the old champagne factory. He hadn't moved from that place in at least fifteen minutes. I took the lead and motioned for the guys to follow me.

Gradually, the businesses and buildings on Main Street became more and more run-down, until we rode by nothing but rows and rows of crumbling brick buildings, windows open and dark like the open sockets of a skull. Shapes of the homeless or junkies huddled in dark corners and waist-high weeds on the sides of the streets.

As we got closer to the rubble of Ground Zero, I thought of what Charlie had said to me. Of how she and Joel were all alone in the world. She'd made a big leap in trusting me because she didn't trust anyone. But she trusted me now. The weight on my shoulders felt so goddamn immense, I didn't think I'd ever felt anything so heavy.

When I rounded the corner, I eased off the throttle and slowed down as I peered between the holes in a rusted old chain-link fence that went around the perimeter of the old champagne factory. A single streetlamp lit the place, casting a dim yellow glow on the lot strewn with garbage and a few empty dumpsters. But my eyes immediately set on the line of motorcycles set up along the crumbling brick walls. In front of each of them, a rider. I counted ten. Fury.

The one in the middle, Scar, stood over another person who was kneeling, his head bent low to the ground as if praying.

It was the kid. Joel.

With a gun, pointed straight at the back of his skull.

Fuck. This wasn't going to end well. I hoped I was just overreacting; for one time in my life, I'd hate being right. No matter what we did, we'd see bloodshed tonight. And after I'd promised Charlie . . . fuck. I really wish I hadn't promised her. The best I could do was try to limit the damage.

I rolled into the lot with the other men, pissed that they had us caged in by the fence with nowhere to hide. They'd planned it that way. Make us sitting ducks so the Fury could pick us off, one by one.

I stopped with Cullen on my right, Drake and Zain on my left in a line. Two opposing armies, ready for battle.

"Nice of you to show," Scar called out, a smile in his voice. "Figured you'd get our message."

I knew Scar, one ugly motherfucker. I'd forgotten what an asshole he could be. He was no better than Slade or Blaze. Totally bald, he usually wore a bandanna on his head. And he had this long, puckered red scar running from his temple, across his cheek, through his lips, to the other side of his chin. Rumor had it, he'd gotten it in a knife fight as a kid, but all of the Cobras joked he'd probably just cut himself shaving.

He tilted his chin to the sky and the light bounced off the shiny, mottled skin of his scar. It wasn't a laughing matter, though. He looked pissed. Out for blood.

"Let the kid go," I said, looking over at Cullen, finishing up a cigarette. So much for giving up smoking. He looked over at me and touched his side, where his gun was.

"I don't think so," Scar said with a sneer. "That's not the plan."

Some of his guys laughed.

"Yeah. Actually, we've been putting off delivering his sentence, because we thought you and your boys might want to be witness to it. What do you say?"

I pulled out my gun and leveled it at his head. "That ain't a good idea. You do anything to him, I'll fucking put a bullet right through that empty head of yours."

The rest of the Fury pulled out their guns, and next to me, the Cobras did the same. The tension in the air was electric. Somewhere far off, a truck's air brakes squealed through the night.

Scar laughed an evil cackle. "Looks like we've got ourselves a party now. Huh, Cullen? How about this?. You tell your boys to stand down and maybe we'll let you all live, after we kill this traitorous piece of shit."

He kicked Joel in the back, and the kid jumped, his head down, his eyes trained on the ground. His red face tore at something deep inside me, and his skinny body shook life a leaf in the rain. His shoulders slumped, making him looked even smaller and more miserable, and a little boy rather than a grown man.

"You don't have to kill him," Cullen said. "Let him go."

Scar let out a bitter laugh. "I think we do. He wanted to wear our patch, and then he goes and shits all over it. That don't sit well with us. You know that. Right, Zain?"

Zain growled, "Fuck off."

"Oh, don't think we forgot the shit you pulled on us. We're still coming for you. We don't forget."

Scar cocked his gun, and Joel squeezed his eyes shut and let out a yelp. "Don't do it unless you want to die," I ordered.

"I think we're owed a little payback from you guys, don't you boys?" he asked, looking around at his goons. They all nodded like puppets on a string. "After all, I think we all know who's responsible for Slade."

"You don't know shit," Cullen said. "Word out on the street is your club's falling apart."

"Word? You mean from this fucker?" He kicked Joel again, this time in the spine, and Joel lurched forward again, letting out a guttural "Oof!" before choking on his spit.

"Well, he don't know shit. We just had elections, boys. And I'll let you pussies be the first to congratulate me. You're looking at the new Hell's Fury President."

I looked over at Cullen. We'd waited too long. They might've been in shambles a few days ago, but now, they were coming back. They were ready to assemble. To kill. And the first targets on their list?

Every last one of us.

Cullen shouted, "You really think the Fury has it all together? Doesn't look like it to me. Jesus fucking Christ, Scar. You're gonna kill one of your own prospects? How does that look to your other prospects? You fucking killing this kid because he made the mistake of talking to the wrong guys? What makes you think anyone will want to turn Fury again?"

"It'll teach 'em a lesson. Not to fuck with us."

"He *wasn't* fucking with you. He almost killed a couple of our guys because he wanted to prove how committed he was to the Fury. And this is what you do to thank him? Hold a gun to his head?"

Scar laughed. "Bullshit. He's been hanging out with you, Hart. We've seen. We know what all of you've been up to. He's a goddamn traitor. And it ends now."

I tightened my finger on the trigger of my gun and looked over at Cullen for help. Cullen set his jaw, and I could see the wheels in his head turning, trying to gauge the situation and how we could get the kid out in one piece. Was there a way? The rest of us froze, like one single breath would be enough to start World War Three. What the fuck could we do now?

Scar's voice was lower now. "He might've been wearing the prospect patch, but he was never going to become a patched member. Maybe he would've made a better Cobra pussy, but he ain't Fury. He's just a little bitch that we used for our grunt work. He was never going to be one of us."

Then, almost casually, he grinned back at his cohorts, leveled the gun and fired one round, into the back of Joel's head.

Fuck!

A spray of blood, and Joel slumped to the side, his face a mask of death.

A beat of silence. My mind couldn't compute what I'd seen. Like I'd blink and find out I imagined the whole thing.

But Joel was on the ground, motionless. Dead.

I saw red. My jaw tightened, my muscles tensed, and before I could take a breath, I stormed them, firing off round after round, wanting to tear those assholes limb from limb with my bare hands. I heard screaming all around me, and as two men fell in front of me, and I felt bullets whizzing past my head, I realized the screams came from me.

Gunshots erupted from all around me as I charged, and I probably would've been hit, had it not been for Cullen, grabbing me and diving behind a dumpster. I hit the ground hard, my face breaking my fall, skidding against the rough, cracked pavement.

Not waiting to gauge the damage, I slammed another magazine in my piece, and shot again. I wanted to shoot until there were no goddamn bullets left in the world.

My eyes drifted down to the lifeless form on the ground. From here, I could see a dark red pool of blood growing under Joel's head.

Holy fucking hell. I shook with a rage I'd never felt before, my veins pulsing under my skin, hot and ready to explode. This was war. I'd fight it as long as it took to bring every one of those assholes down.

But goddammit. As far as Charlotte was concerned, it didn't matter what happened, from here on out.

I would kill every one of these motherfuckers and avenge her brother's death.

Chapter Twenty-Six

Charlotte

Back at the clubhouse, I could do absolutely nothing but wait.

The two men I'd been left with, Nix and Jet, seemed nice enough. I could see why Hart called them his brothers; they were all peas in a pod. They kept busy working on some cars in the back of the warehouse, offered me something to drink and told me to make myself at home in front of the old television set in the corner of the vast room.

I tried.

I sat on an old, overstuffed sofa, watching some lame eighties sitcom but not really comprehending any of it. After a few minutes, I wondered if the local news might give me some hint as to what was going on, so I flipped the channel. I half-expected to see a lead story about two motorcycle clubs getting into a shoot-out downtown. Maybe a couple of arrests. But at four in the morning, the news wasn't running on regular television; I could only find mostly infomercials and reruns.

Then I checked my phone again. No texts since the last time I checked, ten seconds before. I googled the news online but found nothing of interest.

I got up and paced for the hundredth time toward the door, peering through the blinds on the window. I knew I'd probably hear their bikes before I saw them, since they were loud, but I couldn't wait. As I looked into the darkness, I saw the reflection in the glass of someone behind me.

"You might want to get away from the door," a voice said.

I spun around to see the blond guy, Jet, standing there in a dirty t-shirt, wiping his hands on a rag.

"You don't really think the Fury would risk coming here, do you?" I asked but moved away from the door anyway.

"They have before. They're a bunch of Grade A assholes. I wouldn't put anything past them."

I hugged myself and shivered. He wouldn't put anything past them? So, in other words, there was no telling how low they'd sink. And now Jojo was with them.

Right then, I swore to God that when he came back, I'd never let him out of my sight again. I didn't care if the freaking president of the United States called and demanded that he go to the White House; I'd stand between them and tell him no.

I lifted my fingers to my mouth and started to chew on a fingernail as I walked over to see what he and Nix were doing.

They had three cars back there; gorgeous ones. A Mercedes and two hot red sportscars with logos I didn't recognize because I wasn't much of a fan of cars. They looked expensive. I wondered if they'd been stolen. Based on what Hart said, I knew the Cobras were involved in some kind of borderline illegal activities, but the less I knew, the better. Besides, even if they were up to no good, Hart was the most trustworthy person I'd ever met.

Even though I was worried about both of them, Hart was used to this—the fighting, the danger. He was probably fine out there. But as much as Jojo liked to talk a good game, he was still that scared little kid.

The other guy, Nix, who was bigger than the other, closed the hood on one of the cars and looked at me. "Relax, sweetheart. Did you get a beer?" He motioned to the fridge.

I shook my head. "I'm good."

"They haven't been gone that long."

"Thirty-eight minutes," I said. I lifted my phone again. No messages. "Did any of them text you?"

Nix fished his phone out of his pocket. I didn't understand how he could go without looking at it every two seconds—I couldn't stop. He shook his head. "Not since that last one."

The last one was thirty-six minutes ago, from Cullen, the president, who said they were on their way to the canning district and would be back soon. So, nothing I didn't already know. But so much could happen in the space of thirty-six minutes.

I ripped off a fingernail, too close to the quick and it started to bleed. Sucking the blood from the finger, tasting that coppery tang, I looked for my next victim. But all my fingernails were just as bad. I'd had a bit of a manicure prior to tonight, but in only half an hour, I'd totally destroyed it.

I sighed, thinking of the first time I'd ever seen Jojo. I was only six, and I guess my parents were both off the drugs back then because they were together in the hospital. My mother had called me over, asking, "Does big sister want to hold little Joel?"

I'd agreed eagerly. I had one doll at home, my Raggedy Ann, my favorite plaything. I'd put her in the stroller and walk her up and down the halls outside our tiny apartment building. I'd pretend to feed her and burp her and change her diaper, and even then I couldn't wait to have my own real child.

My mother was beautiful back then. When I thought of her, it was never that last, nightmare day, when she had those dark eyes and her skin was almost green from the drugs. No, it was always the day Jojo was born. She'd even insisted on putting lip-gloss on so she'd look good in the pictures.

We had such a perfect family back then. She was so proud of us. I remember climbing onto the bed, into my mother's arms, and she'd prop that little bundle in the blue hat into my arms. And at that moment, I fell in love. All those dreams I'd had about having my own baby? He fulfilled them. I didn't need my doll anymore.

I had my baby brother.

That was the last time we were a family, but I didn't believe it was the last time Joel and I would ever be happy. My parents didn't kill our dreams when they drove away from the Circle K that day. We'd made our own happiness without them. It was hard, sometimes short-lived, and maybe it wasn't the same as if we'd had parents, but we had happiness.

And we'd have plenty more happy times. I was sure of it.

Hart would take care of Joel. He'd continue to take him under his wing and treat him like a brother, and Jojo would flourish. I knew it. Even in the short time my little brother had known Hart, he'd started to change for the better, becoming more of a man, showing an interest in getting a job and taking on responsibility. He'd be fine. Everything would be okay.

I sat back down on the couch as the new morning sun began to filter in through the blinds, a hazy, warm peach, coming up on nearly six o' clock. If they were much later, I'd have to leave—catch an Uber or maybe get one of his friends to take me back home so I could feed the animals. The poor little creatures had to wonder what had happened to Jojo and me.

I smiled, thinking of our plan to get away to Santa Cruz. Maybe, if things went well, Hart would want to come with us. My silly dream, I knew. Hart had made it clear how much the Cobras meant to him. But I couldn't help fantasizing how incredible it would be.

The three of us could start a new life up there, get an apartment together, ride the rollercoaster every night, and not ever have to worry about bullies with names like Scar and Sludge or whatever.

We could have a future together in Santa Cruz.

As I was sitting there, lost in the daydream, sucking the dried blood off my stinging fingertips, I heard the roar of bikes outside—first very soft, but growing louder and louder by the moment. I jumped up, and as the sound became almost unbearably loud, I scrambled to the door.

It swung open as I reached it, and the men filed in, ripping their helmets off, carrying the scent of motor oil, sweat, and gasoline.

They slogged to the table in their ripped and dirty shirts. Some of them blood-soaked. All of them breathing heavy, yet none of them spoke.

And not one of them looked at me. Why were they avoiding me?

I scanned from one to the next, looking for Hart and Jojo. My heart jammed in my throat as Cullen, the president, swept past me. I grabbed his arm. "Where's Hart?"

He tossed his helmet down on the counter and pulled out a pack of cigarettes. He motioned with his chin toward the door.

Hart stood in the doorway, his big frame taking up much of the available space. I could see his chest heaving with every breath through his thin t-shirt. His face was shadowed, so I couldn't see his expression. But thank God. He was here. He was okay.

"Hart," I breathed, running to him. I wanted to smack him for not being the first through the door. He'd worried me. "How did—"

But when I got closer and saw his face, I knew something was wrong.

Blood flowed from an awful gash on his forehead, down the side of his face and ear, drenching the collar of his t-shirt. But he didn't seem to care. His hands, wrapped around his helmet, gripped until his knuckles turned white. His lips twitched, like he wanted to speak, but didn't have the words. And his eyes were full of something I instantly recognized, because I'd seen it so many times before on so many people who'd failed me and Jojo during our lives.

Regret.

His eyes said it all. They encapsulated all of my worst fears. But I refused to believe it. He was wrong. He had to be wrong.

I nudged him aside, to grab Jojo and shake his bony little shoulders and ask him why the hell he'd been so stupid, letting those assholes have their way with him. I'd tell him that the next time any of them called or came around him, I wanted to speak to them. I'd tell them all to go to hell.

But Hart was the last through the door. Jojo wasn't behind him.

I froze there, afraid to turn back. Afraid that I'd see them all looking at me and confirming that it was true.

But I had to know.

And the second I turned around, I wish I hadn't. One of the men—I don't know who—shook his head. He murmured, "I'm sorry," so quietly, it sounded like a prayer.

No. This wasn't happening. This was a nightmare, and I'd wake up. I crossed my arms, hugging myself, but I also started pinching myself, too. Hard. *Wake up, wake up, wake up, Charlotte! WAKE UP!*

It didn't do any good. My knees wobbled and threatened to cave under me. My heart just stopped. Everything inside me did the wrong thing.

"No," I whispered, shaking my head, saying the one word that had crowded out all the others. "No, no, no . . ."

"Charlotte," Hart murmured, his eyes not leaving mine.

When I started, I couldn't stop saying it. But it only got louder, and faster, and now I was screaming it. Screaming and hating, my raw fingernails now claws, ready to tear at anyone who came near me.

Hart made the mistake of trying to comfort me. He put his arms on me but I shook them off. I shoved him, hard, harder than I knew I had in me, and it did more than I expected because he stumbled back, slamming into the door.

"Don't you fucking touch me!" I screamed.

Behind me, dead silence. All the men looking on, watching my life coming to an end. They all just stood there like statues. Like stupid fucking statues that I wanted to knock down and destroy, just like they'd destroyed me.

Because these assholes—with their cool bikes and their tough attitudes and their stupid clubs—had taken away everything on this earth that meant something to me.

And I needed to bring him back.

I reached for the door.

"Where are you going?" Hart said suddenly.

"To get Jojo. I knew I couldn't count on you. Why would you just leave him there like that?" I said bitterly, throwing the door open.

Before I could get myself outside, he put a hand on the door, slamming it shut. "No. Charlotte. We—"

I pummeled his hand, with my fist. "Get. Away. I've got to go. I can't believe you just—"

"He's gone, Char. Listen to me." He grabbed me, settling two heavy hands on my shoulders. I wriggled to get away, but I was no match for him. He held me tight and forced me to look up into his eyes. "Joel's gone. He's gone."

I looked up at him. I couldn't breathe. I was suffocating. My body rebelled at the news—as if one half of my heart had given up, and now the rest of it was following suit. "You left him."

He shook his head. "I didn't. I—"

"Where is his body? I want to see him! If he's dead, I want to see him!" I shouted, wriggling out of his hold. "You left him there? In some dirty fucking alley in the canning district, all alone? Is that what you do to people? Just let them rot like that? That's sick!"

"The Fury were shooting at us. We had to—"

"I don't fucking care!" I shouted, shoving his chest hard. "That's not the way you treat people! He's a person. He's my baby brother. And he's so good. So so so good. He doesn't . . ." I couldn't speak anymore. I just sobbed. I tried to speak but all that came out was a strangled sob.

I grabbed onto the door, yanked it open, and this time I managed to escape his reaching hands and run away. Into the outside world, where there was no one, abso-fucking-lutely no one waiting for me.

Chapter Twenty-Seven

Hart

This was a fucking nightmare.

Of course she'd want to see her brother. He meant everything to her. But it was ten of them against the four of us, and we knew they outnumbered us. We'd barely managed to escape that hole with our lives.

Yeah, it felt like shit, leaving the kid. He didn't deserve to die like that, alone, in that shithole, with no one around him who cared. But there was nothing we could do. I'd go back once the Fury left, but by now, the police were probably swarming the place.

That was why I let her lay into me. I deserved much worse than what she could do to me. I'd promised her, and I'd failed. I let him down, and I'd let her down. I deserved the worst. Not Joel.

When she got done pummeling me, her face ruddy with tears and her hair flying wildly, she tore free, pulling open the door and racing outside.

Behind me, Cullen, nursing a nick from a bullet that grazed his shoulder, said, "Let her go. She just needs time."

Fuck that. She had no way home and wasn't thinking straight. She was liable to do something crazy, like launch herself off the pier.

I didn't think the Fury would come after her now. They'd gotten the best revenge, on all of us. No need to go after the sister, now that Joel was dead. They'd spanked us; no doubt about it. Now, it was our move.

On the way home, the desire to rip their heads off hadn't softened. It'd only grown, multiplied, festered. But looking at Charlotte, I felt like the biggest fucking piece of shit, ever. But, that wouldn't bring him back. That wouldn't make things all right for Charlie. That's all I wanted. And it wasn't possible.

I chased after her, the least I could do was stay with her. Try to make sure that she was safe until she could process the news. I found her at the end of the pier, looking out over the ocean. I scratched at my forehead, because the skin felt tight and itchy, and only then did I realize I had a gash from diving under the dumpster to escape the flying bullets. I was bleeding pretty bad, probably needed stitches, but at that moment, nothing else mattered. I crept up behind Charlie and stood next to her, trying to think of something to say. Something to make it better.

Was there anything?

Hell. No. I'd done a lot of shitty things in my life to people, but this was the worst. My throat tightened and for a second I wished I'd let one of the Fury's bullets get me, instead of Joel. I deserved it more than he did. I should've been in that spot, not him.

"Tell me what happened," she said after a moment, hugging herself in the cool breeze coming off the water. She shivered, covering her pale limbs in goosebumps.

"You really want to know?"

She nodded. "Yes."

"Why? It won't—"

"You don't get it. I know everything about him. *Everything.* I think I deserve to know how he died."

It was the last thing I wanted to talk about. I exhaled and tried to get the explanation over as soon as possible. My tongue felt weighed down by lead as I spoke.

"We got to the parking lot in one of the abandoned factories in the canning district. The Fury had boxed us in, and Scar was holding Joel. We tried to get him to let him go, but he wouldn't. Then he shot him and all hell broke loose. There was nothing we could do."

She swallowed. "Did he . . . say anything before he died?"

I wished I could tell her he had. That his last words were about her and how much he loved her. She needed to hear that right now. Needed to have some little bit of hope to hold onto. But real life isn't like the movies. I shook my head.

"Did they say why? Was it because they found out he'd been talking to you?"

Her voice was so weak. She was going to go over this until she made herself feel as bad as possible. I muttered, "No. They said they were just playing with him. They were going to kill him, no matter what happened."

The fucking assholes. If only he'd come to us first. We could've made him a Cobra, made him a man, so the Fury never would've thought about fucking with him. But he was dead. I had to stop thinking about the what if's.

She put a hand to her mouth. "Yeah. Well, that kind of makes sense, doesn't it? We've been used all our lives. I knew he wasn't one of them. He was too good for them. I only wish he knew it, too, and didn't try to be something he clearly wasn't." Her voice faded away, and she sniffed and wiped her nose with the back of her hand. "Did he . . . was he scared?"

Yeah, he was. And it wasn't because he was a pussy little kid, either. Even the strongest of men would've been pushed over the edge if they'd been in his shoes. It was a fucking awful way to go, with a barrel of a gun to the back of his head, never knowing when the bullet would come and rip off his skull. I knew if I lived to be a hundred, I'd never forget that image—or him. It was burned in my head. I couldn't tell her that. "It happened really fast. He didn't have time to be afraid."

She hung her head, almost like she knew I was lying to protect her, and tears slipped from her cheeks, landing on the boards at her feet. "Was he alone? Did you talk to him before—before—" She stopped and let out a loud sob.

"Like I said, none of us had time. He was gone too quick."

I wanted to wrap an arm around her, but she fisted her hands, tilted her head to the sky and suddenly let out a loud, piercing scream. It was the worst sound I'd ever heard. Then she sank to her knees, covered her face with her hands, and started to bawl.

I put a hand on her shoulder, but she shook me away.

After sobbing for a while, which was pure hell in itself, she sniffled, and wiped at her eyes. "I always imagined something like this would happen. Especially when he started hanging out with the wrong crowd. That's why I was so protective of him. I guess I always knew he was going to leave me. And I didn't want him to go. He's all I have. And now he's gone."

She sounded like a little child. She took a deep breath and looked over at me. "I always thought it'd be a police officer, knocking on my door at three in the morning. Not you." She blew out the air and shook her head. "Not that it matters. Not that anything matters. I did everything in my power to keep this from happening, and it wasn't enough. What a waste."

I shook my head. "No. It wasn't a waste. He knew you loved him, Charlie. He had a lot more than all of us guys have. You really loved him."

"But it's not enough. It wasn't enough to keep him alive."

Overhead, a seagull cried, and she hugged herself tighter. "I need to go," she said after a minute, jumping to her feet, turning her back on the ocean.

Did she want to go home? I couldn't imagine what an ordeal that would be, going back to the apartment she shared with her brother, seeing his room, his things, all traces of his life. How would she handle that? "Where?"

She let out a sad laugh. "Where else? I don't have many choices, Hart. If I did, this wouldn't have happened. If I did, he never would've gotten involved with people like you to begin with."

People like me? So, I was no better than the people who'd ended his life.

Yeah, she was right. I'd fucking lied to her. Betrayed her.

And she wanted me out of her life.

She turned away and mumbled, "Besides, I need to feed my pets."

In all of this, she still remembered her pets. I didn't understand, but then again, I'd never lost anyone that close to me. I searched my mind for the right thing to say but came up blank. I wished she'd just let me hold her, but her posture, arms crossed over her chest, screamed *Stay the fuck away*.

Finally, something came to me. "I can go feed your pets. Why don't you let me take you to my place? You can rest."

"No," she said definitively, as if I'd just offered to take her to hell. "You've done enough. I can just get an Uber."

"You think that's a good idea? You shouldn't be alone."

She stiffened, deliberately avoiding my eyes. "I *am* alone."

"You don't have to be."

"No. Hart. I don't . . . I can't . . ." She shook her head and started to walk away.

I understood. I'd destroyed her trust, taken everything that meant something to her away.

She'd rather be alone than with me. Than with an asshole from a club, just like the clubs who'd taken her precious brother away.

I watched her walk all the way toward the road, her nose buried in her phone, ordering an Uber that would take her away from me.

And I had a feeling it would be for good.

Chapter Twenty-Eight

Charlotte

On my last day of work at the Aveline Bay Veterinary Hospital, my co-workers threw me the party to end all parties. They had balloons and cupcakes and enough fanfare that one would think it was a kid's first birthday party, and the funny thing was, I walked into the cafeteria on my last day of work, having absolutely no clue that any of it was going to happen.

"SURPRISE!" they all shouted as I went inside.

I just stared. I was leaving. Moving on. I wasn't getting married or having a birthday or anything that required a celebration. In fact, I'd been so sad about it, because I really loved the job. But I needed to make a change, and it was the right time.

"We're going to miss you so much," Barb said to me, hugging me. She gave me a little envelope, and when I opened it, my jaw dropped.

It was a check for a thousand dollars. "What is this for?"

"We know things haven't been easy for you in the past few weeks," she said, squeezing my shoulders. "And we understand why you have to leave. But we wish you all the best. And we want you to have a good start."

I needed the money. Joel's funeral had put me in debt. It had also been a wake-up call. After the service, I'd gone home, looked around the apartment we'd shared, and decided that I couldn't be there without him. Immediately, I started to make plans to leave. I found a job at a veterinary hospital just a town over, and it paid even better than my current job. Then I located a little one-bedroom apartment, in a high-rise overlooking the beach. It was almost insane, how easily the pieces fell into place. I only wished Joel could've been there to see it happen.

When I left the Cobra's clubhouse that day, I realized what a lesson in insanity it was, going back to our apartment. Every little piece of it reminded me of him. I had a hundred pictures of him and me on the walls, our entire sordid, fucked up life together He'd left his clothes strewn all over the apartment, and they smelled like him. His whiskers from shaving—the ones I'd always told him to clean up, for fuck's sake—still littered the sink.

I staggered through the place, feeling like I was going to throw up, and then I went to my bedroom and buried myself in the closet, where I couldn't see or hear or smell him. I stayed there all day, until I got a call that night.

From the police.

"We've located a body that we believe is your brother," an officer said. "Can you please come and identify him for us?"

So I did. I had to. I was the only one who could. It was the worst, most awful thing I'd ever had to do. When I looked down on the stretcher and saw what they'd done to him, I sobbed and fell on his body and told him I was sorry for not being a better big sister.

After that, I missed him every goddamn minute of every day. I broke down nearly every ten seconds. The first few days, I stayed in bed all day, wishing I could curl up and die.

Then, I did what I'm best at. I got out of bed, sucked it up, and started taking care of business, planning his funeral.

The funeral was a good thing. The first step to healing. I'd always thought it was just him and me, against the world, but countless people showed up at the funeral to pay their last respects. His friends. His teachers from school. My co-workers. Our neighbors. The service was actually crowded.

And at the funeral, far back by the road, because I didn't think they wanted me to see—a line of men with Cobras on their kuttes, standing in front of their bikes, heads bent respectfully.

They'd left right as the funeral ended, while I fielded hugs and kisses of sympathy. I didn't have a chance to see if Hart was among them. But I imagined he was. He'd probably organized the whole thing.

Hart had been checking on me, in the weeks since. No, he never talked to me, because I never answered his calls, but sometimes I'd hear a motorcycle outside, and when I rushed to the window, I'd see him driving by.

After the funeral, I drove back to the apartment, and it was like I could almost hear Jojo spurring me on. *Get out of here, sis. You know you want to. Just do it.*

So maybe it wasn't Santa Cruz, but it was somewhere where I could shake off the dust. Start a whole new life. And I knew Jojo would be smiling down at me while I did it.

But as I was celebrating the end of this chapter, something very unexpected happened.

In the midst of all the well wishing, I started to get a little hot in that little cafeteria. Stuffy. I had trouble breathing and asked people if they were hot. They all said no, but Barb sent someone to turn down the thermostat. Then, they brought out a cupcake cake, a chocolate one from the bakery down the street that made the *best* desserts. I took one sniff of it, and it hung heavy in my nostrils, like something rotten.

I knew I was going to be sick.

As calmly as I could, I excused myself, went to the rest room, and threw up. I spent the next few minutes, dry heaving over the toilet, then wiped my mouth with toilet paper. After I flushed the toilet, I cupped water from the faucet in my hand and sucked it down. I looked at my sweaty brow and pale complexion in the mirror. The girl that stared back at me was terrified of what this might mean.

I looked up at the ceiling and sighed. *Jojo, if this is your idea of a practical joke, it's not funny.*

I managed to make it through the rest of the party, nibbling on chips instead of cupcakes, and sipping lots of water, which seemed to settle my stomach. The second my shift ended, I kissed everyone goodbye again and high-tailed it to the nearest CVS.

When I got home, I walked around the maze of disarray that was my half-packed apartment. The animals were having fun with the new décor, and Opie curled up to nap in one of the cardboard boxes. I took a second to pet them, then went into the bathroom, read the instructions on the box, and peed on the wand.

Two minutes later, I had my answer.

I was pregnant.

I walked out of the bathroom, stunned, and collapsed on the sofa. "Not funny, Jojo," I said aloud, as Bert jumped onto my lap. I started to stroke his fur. "Not funny at all!"

All right, so this threw a big wrench in my plans. But that was okay. I was a survivor. I'd make it work. I lifted my phone out of my purse and noticed I had a missed call. From Hart, again. For at least the tenth time.

You know you should call him. He needs to know this. Jojo's voice, again. And he was right. I couldn't keep something this big from Hart. He deserved to know.

So I picked up the phone and punched in a call to him. He answered even before it had started to ring. "Charlie?"

My heart twisted. Once upon a time, I may have hated that nickname, but not anymore. His voice struck a chord deep inside me. "Hi, Hart." I took a deep breath. "What are you up to?"

He paused before saying, "I'm at the garage. How are you doing?"

"Okay. I'm all right," I said, as Ernie came by and crawled onto my lap. I gnawed on my lip. "I was wondering . . . can I come over there? I want to talk to you."

Even though he'd been trying to get in touch with me, my heart still hammered in my throat. I'd been ignoring him for a long time, trying to heal. Well, more than a few times I'd gotten the urge to call him, but I'd always suppressed it, reminding myself that associating with people like Hart had gotten Jojo in trouble, ended his life.

As I sat there, waiting for his response, I told myself it would be fine if he didn't want to talk. I'd be better off. I'd survive, even as a single mom, in a strange place, on my own. I always had.

Deep down, I didn't believe that I'd be better off without him. It was Jojo's voice that always came in, whenever I tried to tell myself that. *He's not like those Fury guys. I told you. He's a good man.*

"I'm just getting off my shift," he said after a few minutes, his voice sounding hard and emotionless. "I can swing by your place."

"Oh. Sure. That's good. Thanks."

"See you."

He ended the call and I looked around. The place was a pigsty, but I couldn't do anything about it. I scrambled to the bathroom mirror and splashed water on my face and brushed my hair back into a ponytail.

Only a few minutes later, I heard the sound of his bike coming into the parking lot. I took a deep breath and fixed my hair again, then looked at Ernie and Bert, who were probably wondering what I was so nervous about.

"I'm not nervous," I insisted to my silent little audience, with their droopy little sad eyes, but then I opened the door before he'd even knocked.

Hart stood leaning against the doorframe; fist raised to knock on the door. He dropped it. The light of the streetlamps behind him shadowed his face so I couldn't read his expression. "In or out?" he said in a low voice.

I always wanted him in, no doubt about that. I pushed the door open a little and he took a step closer to me.

I knew he'd come directly from work and hadn't cleaned up yet. He had streaks of grime up his thick forearms, and smudges of grease turned his white t-shirt black. A light sheen of sweat coated his face, and he still had a thick red scar over his eye from a month ago, giving him a perpetually raised eyebrow asking a question.

He looked around my mess of a living room. I'd been working on it for a week straight and still hadn't managed to get everything packed. *And* I still had to bring myself to go through Jojo's room. I'd kept the door closed, so that if I didn't think too hard about it, I could almost believe he was in there sleeping. Every time I thought about going through his stuff, my heart clenched in my chest.

"You're leaving?"

His eyes seemed to scrutinize every last thing in the room, silently judging me. "Yes. I got a job in Baldwin. Up the coast. I thought I'd move closer to it."

"It makes sense. Baldwin's not so far from here."

It wasn't. Just ten miles north. But those ten miles would make a difference. I wouldn't constantly see the street where I taught Jojo to ride a bike or his elementary school or the Jack in the Box where he used to work. "I figured I could do with a fresh start."

"That also makes sense." He hadn't moved from the door.

"Sit down?"

"Sure." He navigated around the boxes and sat down on the sofa. As he did, Bert piled on top of his lap, yawning like he'd found his new bed. Hart didn't make a move to remove him. In fact, he started to pet him, gently, like an old pro. "You wanted to see me?" He put his feet up on the coffee table. "I'm here."

I nodded and came up with what was probably a grim smile as I sank down on the other side of the couch. "Yes. I just wanted to let you know that I don't blame you for anything that happened, where my little brother was concerned. It's not your fault. He liked you. You looked out for him. That's more than a lot of people would do. So, I guess . . . thank you."

He sucked in a breath and let it out. "You raised a good kid, Charlie. I'm really sorry that it happened the way it did. But we're not letting it go. The Cobras, I mean. The Fury have shit on us enough and we're done. We've voted to take out the Fury. Whatever we have to do, we're not going to stop. We have to avenge Joel's death."

I shuddered. "I don't want anyone else to get hurt. They deserve whatever happens to them, but . . . what about you?"

He leaned over and touched my knee, giving me a surly little look that made my nipples stand at attention. "I'll be all right. But thanks for caring." He sucked in a breath and let it out, yawning, looking around at the bare walls. "That what you wanted to tell me?"

"Um . . . well . . ." I bit the inside of my cheek. I realized I hadn't prepared. I wasn't sure how to say this. *I'm pregnant!* – just like that, seemed like a real conversation killer. Plus, I was moving away to another town. And he and the Cobras were getting into a war. And that was the last thing I needed—to bring a baby into a world of violence. That was asking for an outcome like what had happened to Jojo. This was impossible. "I guess."

He studied me. "You sure?"

No. God, no! I could almost hear Jojo's voice echoing with mine. *Tell him. He'll be a good father, and you know it. Then go and jump him.*

I rolled my eyes. I could just imagine Jojo saying that. And I most definitely was not going to jump anyone.

As much as I kind of wanted to.

But then he stood up and started to walk to the door, and I saw my life flash before my eyes. Actually, I saw the life I hadn't lived yet—years and years of *not* being with Hart, spending every single one of those long days filled with regret over letting him go.

It was such a painful thought, I gasped aloud.

Then I shot up, like a bullet fired into the air, and followed after him. "Um, actually . . ."

But stupid me, I didn't realize Mags was under my feet. I went flying again, this time, in a total free-fall, with only Hart's hard body to break my fall. I was on a collision course with his broad back and massive biceps.

Luckily, he turned around at that moment and caught me in his arms. "Whoa," he said, lifting me upright, a small, amused smile cracking on his lips.

I blushed furiously.

"I thought you never trip?" he gritted out in a sexy voice, making me tremble with a need that went deep into my bones.

God, he was so beautiful. So dirty and raw and beautiful, with his light blond hair falling in his face and those incredible hazel eyes, showing all their amber flecks in the orange lamplight. I had no doubt that if the baby inside me had inherited even the tiniest smidgen of his traits, he or she would be a little heartbreaker.

I leaned into his hard muscles, drank in the scent of motor oil, and decided right then and there that there was no way I could let him go. Running my tongue over my lips, I traced a finger over his eyebrow, over the scar. I was quivering like jelly. "You got this that day. Because of Jojo. It makes you look tough."

I let my finger linger there, lightly, until he snatched it in his big hand. He kissed the tip of my finger, then lifted me into his arms. I let out a little squeal as he said, "You're in danger here. That much is clear. If I've gotta save you from yourself . . ."

He carried me in his arms back to the couch, where he sat down with me on his lap. "If you insist on saving me," I said lightly.

He raised that scarred eyebrow in a bigger question. "So you don't want me to leave?"

I shook my head. Then I took a deep breath, and I let it out. "I'd be lying if I let you go. Because I love you, Hart."

He didn't say anything for a long time. It was probably only seconds, but it felt like forever. My heart beat a thousand times in that span of time, as he gazed at me with his sexy eyes. I couldn't tell if they were full of regret or need. What was going on in that beautiful head of his?

Finally, he said, "I kept calling you because I wanted to make sure you were okay. I drove by. You probably didn't know that."

I did. Maybe it was weird, but I swear I could feel him when he was near.

"I wanted to tell you something. But I wasn't going to push my way in if you weren't ready."

I shifted in his lap, feeling his erection against my ass. I braced myself. "Okay. I'm ready now."

His gaze travelled from my eyes, to my nose, to my lips, taking me in, before reaching and holding my eyes again. "I love you, too, Charlie. I don't want to be without you. I know you said you're alone, but you're not. I'll always want you. You got that?"

I cupped his stubbled jaw in both hands. "Do you mean that?"

"Hell, yes," he growled out in a rough voice that just about soaked my panties. He wrapped his arms around my waist, nuzzling my neck with his nose, skimming over my throat with his mouth. Reaching behind my head, he slowly pulled my hair free of the ponytail and tossed the tie away. My hair spilled over us as he gently nibbled on my neck. "Hell. Fucking. Yes. God, you smell so good. I want to fucking eat you right here."

I could have died right then and been as happy as a clam. But I had another life to think about. And it was time. The moment of truth. "But will you want both of us?"

He lifted his head up from the veil of my hair, and his face slowly filled with understanding. His brows came together when he said, "Both of you?"

I nodded and looked down at my tummy.

The corner of his mouth lifted up in a boyish smile. "Shit. Of course, I will." He touched my stomach. "You're not even kidding me?"

His voice cracked a little, which was probably the cutest thing I'd ever heard. Hart, for once, was nervous and excited and totally off his game. I shook my head.

"Hell, yes, I'll want both of you. Forever."

"But . . ." His eyes widened from the news as he raked his hands through his hair and looked around at all my boxes. "Shit. You're moving away from me."

"Well, I . . ." All I knew was that I didn't want to stay in the apartment I'd shared with Jojo. "Like I said, not far. I got an apartment on the beach in Baldwin. I'm supposed to move in next month."

"You sign a lease? Give in a security deposit?"

I shook my head. "Not yet."

"Then move in with me. Baldwin's not far from my place."

I blinked. "But . . ." Actually, that would be perfect. Me and him, and all his little tinker toys. My eyes trailed to Mags, sniffing Hart's boot. "What about my pets?"

"Bring them," he said with a shrug, tightening his thick arms around me. "I fucking love animals."

I smacked his hard chest. "You do not!"

"I'll learn to. If it means I can wake up next to you every morning, hell. I'll be a fucking cat lady, if you want me to be."

"No. I just want you to be you." I grinned at him, so sure Jojo was watching over us, happy and excited for what we had. For what we would have. I laced my fingers with his as he kissed my mouth, savoring my lips. "If he's a boy," he murmured against my mouth, "We'll name him Joel. Okay?"

"Yes, that's perfect," I said.

"A girl, she can be Josephine," he breathed out, moving along to my chin, setting little nibbling kisses along my jaw. His hand reached under my camisole and caressed my belly. "Either way, it'll be our Jojo."

"I like that," I said to him, wrapping my arms tightly around his neck.

And I could feel it. No, I couldn't just feel it. I knew it. Knew it with everything that I was, with more certainty than I'd ever known anything.

Jojo liked it, too.

The End

Acknowledgements

Thank you so much for reading my books! I appreciate you so much. Without you, I couldn't do what I do.

Thanks to KB Winters for dragging me along this journey. And extra special thanks to all my FB fans, ARC readers, editors and everyone who helps me get to publish my books. You know who you are and I love you for it.

Thank you!

Evie

EVIE MONROE

About The Author

I love fairytales, princesses and bad boys. I just didn't realize how much until I started writing about them. I have found a new love in my life and I hope you have too!

You can find all of my books at EvieMonroe.com

facebook.com/eviemonroeauthor/

eviemonroeauthor@gmail.com

eveimonroe.com

Made in the USA
Coppell, TX
22 February 2023

13282744R00225